# Merry in Moonvale

# Merry in Moonvale

## MOONVALE MATCHES
### BOOK 2.5

## HAILEY BLACKWOOD

THE REALM OF ALDOVA
Dragonspear Mountains
Tidegrove
Sunhaven
Ash Hills
Rockward
Willowvalley
River of Wishes
Kingston
The Barren Lands
Oakhollow
River of Hope
River of Lost
Moonvale
Starshore
Greenwood Forest

*Because your favorite characters deserve to have a happy holiday, too.*

Author's Note

I want to make sure everyone is FULLY aware: **Merry in Moonvale**, while cozy and stress-free, does contain themes that might be upsetting to some readers.

You can expect:
- Adult Language
- Explicit Sexual Content
- Very Mild Mentions of Injury/Blood
- Alcohol

**This novella occurs after the events of *Love Letters & Thirst Tonics* and *Cauldrons & Cat Tails*. For the full experience, those should be read first.**

You may proceed. (:

# CHAPTER 1

# *Kizzi*

A crisp, icy wind flowed through the open window of my apothecary shop, smelling of frost and burnt sugar. It caressed my skin with a frigid kiss and tossed my hair across my face, the strands dragging through my eyes and temporarily blinding me.

I hastily brushed my green bangs back with dust-covered fingers.

And then a small weight settled onto my shoulder, hot enough to nearly singe the fabric of my blouse. I flicked it off immediately. Dust plumed from my filthy hands. "Gods, Scarlett, I told you to stop doing that! You're going to catch me on fire!"

The tiny fire sprite hovered a few inches in front of my face, arms crossed and steam puffing from her ears in small, wispy tufts. "It's not my fault you're so fragile, Godsblood. It never bothered you before."

Godsblood. Ugh. It was the name the sprites had refused to stop calling me, even though it didn't make any sense.

I didn't care for an explanation. What they had to say about it was impossible. And absolutely fucking ridiculous.

I had accrued too many new aliases lately. Godsblood, assigned to me by the sprites. Hand of the Dragons, assigned to me at the witch over in Rockward. I missed being just Kizzi. Kizziah Cedarton, Moonvale's favorite apothecary witch. And nothing else.

"It's Kizzi. I told you that. You *know* that."

Scarlett nodded solemnly. "Whatever you say, Godsblood."

I rolled my eyes. "What do you want?"

Scarlett wrung her hands in front of her, her transparent wings fluttering rapidly. "Can you close the window?"

I pointedly held up my dust-covered hands, gesturing to the worktable in front of me. It was a mess. I had been smashing up quartz crystals, collecting the dust in jars for later use in my potions.

I had a new idea for a potion that might free the dragons from their impenetrable shells.

"I need to keep them open, sprite, or the dust will clog our noses and kill us all. Is that what you want?" That was a complete lie. I knew it, but they didn't.

A chorus of small gasps echoed around the shop reflecting varying levels of horror.

"No!"

"Did she really say that?"

"We can't kill the Godsblood!"

I could've sworn one of them actually burst into tears.

I chuckled quietly to myself. The sprites were easy to rile up. They spent years tormenting me, so it was poetic that I could now torment them right back.

Really, I was just keeping the window open to appreciate a few final dredges of fresh air. The freeze season was in full swing, and temperatures were plummeting, though it wasn't miserable yet.

But it would be soon.

With the freeze season came one shining perk: Merry Day —a holiday celebrated throughout the entire realm, where friends and neighbors took an entire day off to relax, be happy, and occasionally, exchange gifts. I had yet to start preparing, much to my best friend Fiella's dismay.

Scarlett dimmed, settling onto the edge of my new cauldron and tucking her legs beneath her. "The window must stay open. I was just a little cold, that's all. My flames don't like the wind. But your safety is more important."

Guilt prodded at my insides.

It was easier to mess with the sprites before. Before I'd softened to them. Before they'd stolen crumbs of my heart.

Before we could speak to each other.

Now, they never *stopped* speaking.

A handful of weeks had passed since magic had mysteriously returned to the realm of Aldova. Since the sprites had become more creature than wisp. Since they'd grown into tangible beings that could converse like any other folk.

Only weeks since everything had changed.

It was inconvenient, being soft.

With a heavy exhale through my nose, I drifted to the window, pulling it most of the way shut so only the tiniest of drafts could pass through. Though Scarlett objected, I could see the way her posture relaxed to a more comfortable position, how she brightened back to her normal orange color, and how other sprites began stirring again.

Annoyingly, it pleased me. I had grown to like when my apothecary felt full of life.

Not all of the sprites were brave enough to speak out in the open.

Scarlett was—the tiny fire sprite was brave but always irritatingly polite. And there was an outspoken water sprite, too. Dropp, her name was. There was also a wind sprite named Thrum who was never afraid to voice his opinions, but he was grumpier than the others. Moodier. He sulked in a dark corner just as often as he openly glowered.

The others were slowly coming around.

Hex, too, was coming around.

My purple cauldron sludge familiar that I had accidentally brought to life was now practically glued to me at all hours of the day.

Hex, in their gelatinous form, could often be found perched on my shoulder, slumped beside my ankle, or simply watching me from the broken cauldron they had claimed as their own. I still wasn't sure what to expect from my new familiar. Old legends spoke of familiars as powerful creatures that strengthened and stabilized their witch. That were steadfast and strong, brimming with magic.

Mostly, mine just annoyed me. And stole my snacks whenever they thought I wasn't looking. They had helped me on Hallow's Eve, sure, but they hadn't done much else.

They still made me shiver. Especially when I caught an unexpected glimpse of them from the corner of my eye.

Thinking about Hex prompted me to glance over my shoulder to the broken cauldron in the corner.

They looked... strange. Stiff. Tense.

"Hex?" I called out. "You alright, buddy?"

Hex didn't respond, and they didn't give a telltale gurgle or bubble pop either. That couldn't be good.

I heaved out a sigh. "Hang on. I'm coming."

One thing I had learned about Hex was that they were impressively temperamental. If something unpleasant became stuck to them, they would freeze up like a stone until I came and removed the offending object. It had first happened with a loose strand of my hair. And then later with a small dirty pebble. I wondered what had caused them to freeze up this time.

They could engulf just about anything to sustain themself but when it came to small nuisances... I didn't understand how they worked but I knew that *not* helping would only get me spat on. Or worse.

I drifted to the washbasin to quickly rinse the crystal dust from my hands, dabbed them dry on a towel, and then made my way to the cauldron.

"Alright, Hex. Let's see what's bothering you."

My feet tapped quietly across the wooden floor of the apothecary, joining the muted hush of the sprites conversing with each other and the whisper of wind whirling through the crack in the window.

I was still adjusting to the sound of their voices. It was jarring compared to the silence I had grown accustomed to during the years of them inhabiting my shop.

I grasped the edge of the giant broken cauldron and leaned in to get a good look. Hex was their usual bright, glossy purple color, but instead of being soft and malleable, they were rigid. Like crystal instead of slime.

And they were curled around the three dragon eggs.

Red, blue, and green, the large, scaled eggs were nestled

comfortably in the bottom of the cauldron, as they usually were when I wasn't actively trying to crack them open.

Hex was curled around them, even more protective than usual. It would be endearing if it didn't set the hairs on my arms to standing.

Something about the situation put me on edge.

I reached in and tapped Hex gently, where they met the edge of the cauldron. "Hey, Hex. Are you good? What's the issue here?" My fingernail clicked on their surface instead of sinking in.

I got the impression that they didn't want to move. But I needed them to, if I was going to ease their strange tension.

Quickly, I twisted my green waves back into a knot to keep them out of my face (and out of Hex's surface). And then, cringing, I slipped my fingers between Hex and the cast iron of the cauldron.

"Sorry about this, but I've got to get you out if there is something stuck to you."

They resisted. They *really* resisted. A zap of magic traveled through my fingers, into the bones of my hands, and up my arm. Nausea curled in my stomach at the sensation.

I grumbled under my breath. "Gods be damned. Bitch. Don't attack me, I'm just trying to help."

They resisted harder, liquifying for just a moment so my hand jerked through their surface and nearly smacked my own face.

I rolled my eyes. "Fine! Be miserable then. Insolent familiar. You're supposed to follow *my* rules."

They gurgled, clearly annoyed, which was a pile of shit because *I* was the one who should be annoyed.

"Don't come crying to me next time you have fuzz on your face, then. Brat."

A bizarre stab of worry tore through my chest, nearly doubling me over. I rubbed my collarbone to ease the sensation.

With one last glance (glare) at Hex in the cauldron, I turned to finish up my latest concoction.

But the worried sensation intensified.

My palms broke out in a clammy sweat, and a cold shiver straightened my spine, entirely different than the cold drifting in through the window. This was the cold of fear, of despair, of anxiety.

I wished Tandor was here. My mate might have been a softie when it came to some things, but he always soothed my worries and eased my fears.

"What is it, Hex? If you won't let me help you, then at least let me get back to work."

My stomach tied itself in a knot.

Fighting the nausea, I returned to the cauldron, to my annoyingly needy familiar.

"Fine. You win. What do you want me to do?"

I waited. Slowly, Hex loosened from around the dragon eggs, exposing them fully to my view.

What I saw made me squint my eyes and question my sanity.

I leaned in, bracing my hips on the rim of the cauldron and bringing my face within inches of the red dragon egg. It was shiny, with an indescribable shimmer that could only be magical in origin. Swallowing down my nerves, I reached out trembling fingers.

There was a small, black line decorating the surface of the

dragon eggshell. The scaled surface made the line difficult to identify, but it was certainly *something*.

I ran my fingertips over the surface, entirely prepared for the black line to be one of Hyacinth's hairs, a local witch with long black locks. But it didn't brush aside. A tiny, almost imperceptible divot could be felt along the black line.

My brain struggled to put the pieces together.

Fiella and I had been trying for weeks to crack the dragon shells open. And not just the two of us. Tandor tried, too, with his orcish strength. And Fiella's mate, Redd, who had all sorts of woodworking tools at his disposal. And a few of the witches that we could trust to keep the eggs a secret from Mayor Tommins.

We worked relentlessly. We had tried potions. Tonics. Flames. Ice. Rituals. Brute force. Nothing had worked.

But now, impossibly, a small crack marred the egg's surface.

I barely noticed the weight of a sprite settling on my shoulder, grabbing onto my tunic for stability. My mind whirled.

This was what Hex had wanted me to see.

The dragons were finally hatching.

My heart thundered in my ears, my jaw unhinging and hanging open.

I dipped, planting a quick smacking kiss to Hex's surface before yanking myself upright and flying to the door.

"Fiella!" I screamed. "It's happening!"

CHAPTER 2

*Fiella*

My fingers ached with an unfamiliar throb as they struggled to find a firm grasp on the bundle of yarn I was holding. The strands were impossibly slippery.

Merry Day was great, sure, but the gift part was absolutely kicking my ass.

Embarrassingly, I was trying to learn how to knit. It was not going well.

The instructional book was not helpful enough, making the steps seem easy and fluid. Knitting was the opposite of easy. My fingers refused to cooperate, and the knitting needles weren't doing their job, either.

I grumbled under my breath as I untied yet another knot. "Fucking fates. How do folk do this? Why can't I just buy scarves and sweaters—why do I need to make them?"

A deep laugh rumbled out of Redd's chest. He sat in a stuffed chair in the corner of my trinket shop with a book propped on his lap. "Nobody's stopping you from buying the sweaters, love. You're the one who decided you were going to

9

make them. Just because Kizzi and Tandor are making gifts this year doesn't mean you have to."

"Shut up. You're supposed to be on my side," I grumbled. My fingers snagged in the yarn. Again.

He was right, though. As he usually was. I knew I could find something in my trinket shop for all of my friends and family. I could give some beautifully woven baskets to Kizzi, some rare oak wood relics to Redd, and some flower vases to Lunette, and so on. And I probably would, if I couldn't get this damned yarn to cooperate.

Kizzi and Tandor were making gifts because they had blown through all of their silvers on a journey across the realm, when they purchased the dragon eggs.

But something about a handmade gift felt more full of love. More special.

And I had set my mind on knitting my gifts—a choice I was now regretting.

"You can do this, Fiella. Just be patient. You'll get the hang of it." Redd closed his book with a gentle thud and set it on the table in front of him, slowly rising to his feet. I glanced at him from the corner of my eye.

He never failed to take my breath away. His easy, lethal grace. The way his muscles perfectly hugged his bones, granting him both power and stealth. The way his dark brown hair was always a bit tousled, even when he tried to tame it.

And the way his fangs peeked out between his beautiful lips when he smiled at me, as he was doing now when he caught me peeking at him.

He drifted behind me where I was perched on my stool, stroking his hands over my shoulders and down my arms, stopping before he met my hands or interrupted my handi-work. He knew better.

He rested his chin on my shoulder and pressed a quick kiss to my cheek. I softened in his embrace, some of my stress melting away.

His voice was molten, so close to my ear. "Need my help?"

I sighed and fought the shiver that worked down my spine and the way his proximity heated my blood. "You want to help me knit?"

He shook his head, and his short beard snagged on a few strands of my hair, disturbing it where it laid over my shoulder in blue rivulets. "No. I'd be no help with that. I can help you with other things, though."

This piqued my curiosity. "Oh?"

Warm hands traced up my arms again, over my shoulders, slipping down to slide around my waist. "I can take your mind off of it, for a moment."

Arousal pooled in my stomach and I leaned into his touch, but I kept my hold on the yarn, determined not to lose my place. I groaned in dismay. "Not now. Can't. I'll never finish this in time. Merry Day is only a week away."

Redd tilted his head, pressing a soft kiss where my ear met my neck, a place he knew was one of my weaknesses. I sighed dreamily. "Later, then," he said softly.

I nodded. "Later. Definitely later—" I caught a sound from outside, one that straightened my spine and tightened my muscles. "Did you hear that?"

Redd, too, had heard the chilling sound—probably before I did. We were both vampires, but he had more vampire blood than I did, which strengthened his senses.

I tentatively stood from my stool. Redd drifted toward the front door of Fiella's Finds, quick and silent on his feet.

The sound repeated. Clearer, this time. It was... screaming.

Kizzi screaming.

Immediately, I tossed the wad of yarn and knitting needles aside and rushed to the door, the sound of my best friend's screams immediately flushing my veins with panic.

Redd yanked the door open and stepped aside to let me out first, and then he followed immediately after. The door slammed shut behind him.

"Kiz!" I shouted. "Kizzi!"

The green haired witch was sprinting down the street, huffing and puffing, holding her skirts scrunched up in both fists. She didn't even have a cloak over her tunic. Her skin was flushed and her expression was stretched tight. "Fiella!" she screamed. "It's happening!"

I met her halfway, grasping her shoulders and scanning her quickly, checking for injuries. I glanced behind her to check for a disaster or a pursuer. Everything looked normal. "What happened?"

"It's happening. It's happening!" She reached out with trembling hands and grasped my face, squeezing my cheeks before grabbing my hand and tugging.

"What? What's happening?"

Redd drifted up beside me and crossed his arms over his chest. "Is everything alright?"

"Guys! Listen to me!" Kizzi whipped her head around, frantically scanning the area for other passersby. Nobody was close enough to overhear. "It's the eggs."

My eyes snapped to her face and widened. "No fucking way."

"Yes fucking way!" She tugged on my hand harder. "Let's go!"

I glanced at Redd to find his expression had slackened. He shrugged. "You heard the witch. Sounds important. Let's go."

"Okay. Going. Yes." I finally allowed Kizzi to drag me toward her apothecary. My short friend wasn't very strong, but she was determined.

The chill finally permeated my panic and I longed for my cloak. I shivered and tucked my free arm around myself, sidling up closer to Kizzi.

Dragon eggs topped cloaks. Obviously. But it was still fucking *cold*.

Redd scurried behind us. "Should I grab Tandor?" he asked hesitantly.

"Tandor! Tandor. Yes. He should see this too. But keep it quiet."

"Of course," he agreed. "I know how this has to go." He turned toward Ginger's Pub to retrieve Tandor, where he would be serving ales at this time of day.

We shoved through the door of Kizzi's apothecary.

The sprites were a flurry of movement. It was a shock every time I entered the shop—I didn't know how Kizzi tolerated it. The sprites were overwhelming. There were tens of them. Maybe hundreds. All flying, chattering, scurrying, making a symphony of noises.

It was miraculous, how different they were now that magic had returned. Before, they were simply wisps. Barely there. Hardly noticeable. Now, they were a force to be reckoned with. A sensory overload.

The shop was thrumming with magic. Different from the way the rest of the realm was reinvigorated. I could feel it with every frantic pump of my heart, every sharp inhale of my breath. It was electric.

It was also a little terrifying.

Kizzi tugged me to the cauldron in the corner, the one her dreadful familiar had destroyed when it came to life. I braced myself to see it.

The slimy thing, Hex, freaked me out. It was fucking weird. Even if it was bound to Kizzi's soul like the witches said it was... it certainly could have been cuter.

Hex was spread around the bottom of the cauldron, surrounding the three perfect, beautiful, gorgeous dragon eggs. I had the urge to snatch the eggs away, to protect them from Hex's sliminess, but I knew Hex had grown attached to them. Like a mother hen.

It would have been endearing, if it wasn't so squirm-inducing.

"What am I looking at here?" I asked, trying to keep my distance from the slime.

"*Look!*" Kizzi insisted, shoving me closer.

I sighed. I couldn't avoid the slime forever, it seemed. I leaned in.

The first thing I noticed was how gorgeous the eggs were, as per usual. They were scaled and richly colored. Perfect and beautiful. And so, so powerful. I resisted the urge to gnash my fangs. My protective instincts were in overdrive.

The second thing I noticed was the crack.

I screamed, and the sound startled a few sprites off of their perches. Even Hex flinched reflexively. "No way! No way, no way, no way!"

"I told you! It's happening! The eggs are finally hatching!"

"What do we do?" I asked, only slightly panicking. We had been trying to hatch the eggs for weeks, but part of me thought it would never actually happen. I acted like I expected them to open, of course, but deep down, I never really allowed myself to hope.

And now, it was actually fucking happening. And I had no idea what to do with myself.

"I don't know!" Kizzi shouted, clearly as bewildered as I was.

"You're the Hand of the Dragons, isn't this your entire job?" I asked.

"That's a phony title and you know it!"

"It was given to you by the witch dragon egg saleswoman. It had to mean something."

"Hex won't let me pick it up!"

I huffed. "Hex is your gods damned familiar. Make them."

She glanced at me nervously. "Okay. I'll try. But let it be known that I warned you."

Before she could sink her fingers into Hex's surface, the door flew open. In charged a vampire, an orc, and a faun. Redd had returned, and he brought Tandor and Ginger with him.

Kizzi straightened. "Redd! We told you to grab Tandor!" She glanced at the faun woman. "No offense, Ginny. You know we love you."

Ginger leaned casually against a table, crossing her hoofed feet at the ankle. "No offense taken. But I overheard, and there was no way in Hell's Realm I was going to miss this. I can keep a secret."

Kizzi shrugged. "Fair enough. But brace yourself, it might not be pretty."

Ginger smiled warmly. "Consider me braced. Just let me know if you need another set of hands."

Kizzi reluctantly turned back to the cauldron and started muttering under her breath. "Okay, Hex. I mean it this time. Let me take the egg, or I'll smear you along the cobblestones outside and leave you there to freeze."

A tiny gasp echoed from somewhere overhead. I smothered a laugh.

Tandor and Redd lingered with Ginger a few paces away from the cauldron. Smart folk. They were staying out of the splash zone.

I patted Kizzi's shoulder reassuringly, relieved that the witch was here to spare me from touching Hex myself.

She sunk her hand in. She flinched when her fingers made contact, and then shook her arm as though relieving an ache. I could smell magic drifting off of her in gentle waves. It battled with the charged ice and cinnamon scent of the shop.

She went in again, this time gritting her teeth and pulling her eyebrows down into an impressive glare. If she had fangs, she surely would have been snarling with them. "I. Mean. It. Get. *Off*."

Hex tightened again, nearly obscuring the eggs from view. A swell of panic squeezed my chest.

"Oh, no you don't!" Kizzi gritted out, before using her other hand to send a small bolt of magic into the slime. Immediately, Hex relented, shrinking in on themself and retreating to the corner of the cauldron where they hissed and spat tiny chunks of slime into Kizzi's face. If she noticed, she didn't react—she was too focused on carefully grabbing the red egg and pulling it into her arms.

I let out a strained breath, nearly deflating with the weight of it. I leaned over to drag my fingers over the egg's rippled surface. It sure was a crack. And it wasn't a tiny one, either, barely perceptible like the lines I had previously noticed on the eggs. These were *real* cracks.

Ginger held her breath where she stood, and Tandor nervously shifted his weight. Redd merely observed, calm and stoic.

Kizzi passed the egg to me. It settled in my arms like it belonged there, warm and heavy and almost buzzing with energy. My veins flooded with a feeling somewhere between love and awe, a sensation that I was beginning to associate as uniquely from the eggs. It was innate, like I couldn't help but respect the small dragons. I instinctively knew the critters were more powerful than I could ever dream of being.

It was mind boggling. Not even hatched yet, and the critter already had me wrapped around its little claws.

I tucked the egg more securely into the crook of my elbow.

Quietly, Kizzi murmured soothingly to Hex, trying to seek forgiveness from her familiar. It didn't sound like it was going well.

Tandor drifted over to me, leaning in to get a good look at the egg. "Wow. It really is cracked, huh. That's unbelievable."

"I bet it was my saw that did it," Redd stated from where he stood.

"Sure, my love. I bet it did." But I knew it was more likely Kizzi's doing, or something related to the magic returning to the realm. Or one of the cats, who we had caught clawing at the eggs more than once.

I still could hardly believe it. That magic was back. It didn't feel real.

"What do we do?" I asked nobody in particular.

"Should we pry it open?" Tandor asked. Overhead, I heard a chorus of horrified gasps. The sprites clearly didn't think that was a good idea.

"Maybe you should try a potion, now that it can seep inside," Ginger suggested helpfully. She didn't seem shocked by the situation whatsoever—she had simply hopped on board.

But that idea didn't feel quite right, either. The potions were abrasive and aggressive, and I didn't like the thought of them harming the fragile little dragon inside. We didn't even know if a dragon would be inside the egg, and if so, if they were still *alive*. It seemed impossible, to be trapped for countless years and remain with the land of the living. For all we knew, there could be a tiny sad corpse inside.

But I didn't think so. Somehow, miraculously, I thought magic had found a way to protect the creatures, even during the years when there were only crumbs of residual magic left in the realm. It found a way to cocoon them. To keep them safe.

I didn't want to test that theory too rigorously, though.

"Maybe we should just wait," I said, bouncing the egg gently in my arm as though I were rocking a baby.

"We're running out of time," Kizzi gritted out tightly. "Merry Day is only a week away, and we told the witch at Rockward that we would return the eggs if they didn't hatch by then."

I considered this. "There's still time. We don't have to panic yet. Clearly, *something* is happening. Let's give it a day or two before we take any drastic actions."

And as I said the words, the egg in my arms seemed to tense, to vibrate.

*Crrrrack.*

Slowly, another tiny fissure opened up on the egg's surface.

I couldn't help myself—I screamed.

# CHAPTER 3

# Kizzi

Chaos erupted.

Absolute chaos.

The sprites exploded into motion, panicking in their tiny, shrill voices while they either fled, hid, or simply flew around in a flurry of excess energy.

Casper, the fluffy white cat who had previously been sleeping peacefully in a basket of sheets, strutted into the room, watching the scene unfold with bright green eyes.

Fiella frantically bounced on her feet, clutching the egg with both hands and holding it out in front of her like it would explode.

Which it totally might. We had no idea what was supposed to happen when a dragon egg hatched. There were no helpful texts on the matter.

Ginger ran in circles around the room clutching her antlers, chanting, "Old Gods help us. Old Gods help us," over and over again while her hooves clanked noisily against the floor.

Redd froze where he stood, looking like he couldn't

decide if he wanted to bolt or scoop Fiella up and carry her away.

Hex leapt from the cauldron and raced toward Fiella, who promptly shrieked even louder and ran in the opposite direction.

And Tandor, bless him, joined in the shouting and ran over to me, tucking his body around mine and shielding me as though the building would cave in. I would have been flattered if I wasn't so overwhelmed.

It was madness all around.

Tiny cracks continued, somehow impossibly loud even in the chaos of the room. The crackling, popping sound was deafening.

And then the front door flew open.

Everyone froze where they stood. Except for Hex, who took the opportunity to slink over Fiella's shoe, crawl up her leg, and settle into the crook of her elbow. She looked like she might vomit.

In the open doorway stood Mayor Tommins. The exact folk we were trying to hide the existence of the dragon eggs from.

*Fuck*.

The gryphon looked taller than ever, imposing and regal in his thick cloak and gloves. His mane of golden hair was smoothed back in a bun, and his heavy brows were pulled together in an expression somewhere between confusion and concern.

And he stared at the scene before him.

Nobody moved. Nobody spoke.

The abrupt silence was almost painful, but I refused to

break it, not ready to deal with the consequences of my own actions.

Finally, either seconds or hours later, it was hard to tell, Mayor Tommins spoke. "Kizziah? What's going on here?"

I choked on my words. "Just hanging out with some friends, that's all." I smiled painfully. Tandor loosened his grip on me, straightening into a more natural position.

*Crack. Pop. Pop.*

The gryphon's eyes snapped to Fiella, where she still stood frozen, clutching the egg between trembling fingers with Hex curled around her arm. His eyes nearly bulged from his skull. "And what's that?" he asked.

Fiella gulped. She glanced at me, panicked, but I had no help to provide for her. I merely shrugged. We were doomed. Mentally, I prepared myself for an eternity in the dungeons.

"It's... it's an egg, sir," the vampire mumbled.

Tommins stepped inside, pulling the door shut behind him. A cluster of sprites escaped as he did so. "I can see that. What kind of egg is it? And why is everyone screaming?"

Fiella clamped her mouth shut. When Tommins looked as though he would ask again, Tandor spoke up from where he stood behind me. "It's a dragon egg, sir. I bought it."

I elbowed him in the gut and whirled around to face the tall orc, shocked. Sure, he had helped me pay for the eggs, but the entire situation was my doing. Well, and Fiella's, too. But Tandor wasn't at fault here. And I refused to let him take the fall from me. "No! I was the one—"

It seemed Fiella wouldn't let that happen, either. She spoke over me. "It's my fault, Tommins. I forced Kizzi to buy it for me. This was all my doing."

Tommins' gaze flitted between the three of us, and then

to Redd and Ginger, who had yet to speak up, but looked like they were both prepared to take the blame, as well. If we were going down, we were going down together, it seemed.

My eyes watered up and my throat tightened. I had to swallow before I could speak again. "I bought the eggs, sir. From a witch in Rockward. It's a long story."

Tommins stared for a moment before he spoke again. "You brought a dragon egg to Moonvale. A real dragon egg."

I pointedly avoided looking at the broken cauldron in the corner, where the two other eggs rested. "Yes. I did."

"And you didn't run this by me?"

I nervously smoothed my skirts. "No, I didn't."

"And why is that?"

"I didn't want you to take them away from me. I couldn't risk it."

*Crack. Pop. Pop.*

"Hmm. And now..." he trailed off.

Fiella spoke up. "And now, it appears to be hatching."

"Hatching," Mayor Tommins repeated, dumbfounded. "It's hatching. A dragon egg."

Fiella nervously shifted her weight, adjusting her quaking fingers to find a firm grip on the cracking shell. "It would appear so."

"Old Gods almighty," Tommins breathed. "A dragon. Here. In Moonvale."

I stepped forward, presenting my wrists to Mayor Tommins so he could shackle them and take me away. "Well, the secret's out. You can lock me up now. I know I'm in trouble."

Tommins glanced at my face before his eyes drifted back to the egg in Fiella's grasp. "Why would you say that?"

I halted. "You—you mean I'm not getting thrown in the dungeon?"

"Of course not. If I didn't throw you in the dungeon for importing toxic plants and outlawed potion ingredients, what makes you think I would for this?"

That stopped me short. He had a point. "I'm not in trouble?"

Tandor let out a heavy sigh of relief behind me, tucking an arm around my waist to tug me back into him.

Tommins tilted his head. "No. Of course not. As a matter of fact, I think I'm offended at the assumption." He glanced around the room. "Did you all think that? Is that why you're all confessing—you thought I'd throw you all in the dungeon?"

Nobody spoke. Fiella coughed awkwardly, while Ginger stared at the floor, and Redd exhaled heavily through his nose.

Tommins stepped toward Redd. "Even you? I thought you knew me better than that," he said, sounding vaguely hurt.

Redd glanced up to meet his gaze. "No. Well, you are the mayor, you're in charge of this town. And dragons are... nobody knew how you would take it."

Tommins straightened, running a hand over the fur trim of his collar. "Oh. Well. No, you're not in trouble. As long as the town stays intact. But seeing as you all thought... I'll just go ahead and leave. Stop screaming. You're causing a commotion."

And with that, he turned and yanked the door open, stepping hastily outside.

As a cold burst of air flooded through the door, three things happened simultaneously.

Hex tensed, and then lunged for the egg, but they weren't fast enough.

Fiella tossed the egg away and then covered her face while Redd reached an arm out to catch her.

And the egg burst open, sending chunks of shell scattering to every corner of the room.

This time, everyone screamed, including Mayor Tommins.

Faster than seemed possible, a tiny creature materialized from nothingness, took flight, and bolted out the open door.

And just like that, the baby dragon hatched, and was gone.

When the screams died down, Tommins turned, fixing me with a hard stare. "And that's your responsibility," he declared. He glanced around the room. "All of you. If that dragon destroys my town, or ruins Merry Day... As you all said, I do have a dungeon below my office, and it's been vacant for quite some time."

*How ominous.*

He left without another word, leaving the door open behind him.

"What should we—"

"Oh, fuck—"

"Old Gods help us—"

Everyone spoke at once. I interrupted them, sending a small flare of magic through the air to catch their attention. They shut their mouths at once.

I curled my fingers into my palms, feeling vaguely embarrassed. I still wasn't used to controlling so much magic.

"Shut up. Get yourselves together. Now let's go catch a baby dragon before it destroys the town."

# CHAPTER 4

# Fiella

It turned out that baby dragons were *extremely* adept at playing hide-and-seek. So much so that even after hours of searching, we couldn't find the newly hatched creature.

It was like it hatched and promptly poofed out of existence.

Still, we kept looking.

We crept through Town Square, peeking under benches and behind shrubs, around tree trunks and in squirrel nests. We poked our heads into shops and peered into cottage windows. We tried to catch a scent trail.

No luck.

We even ventured to the edges of the forest, disturbing piles of fallen leaves and searching through foliage.

The problem was, nobody knew enough about dragons to predict where they might want to hide.

In old legends, dragons typically hatched in the caves beneath the Rockward mountains, far, far away. Dread settled like a stone in my stomach when I considered that the tiny dragon might be on its way to the mountains now, braving the Barren Lands in an attempt to get there.

No. That was too awful to consider. They had to be around here somewhere.

A soothing hand settled onto my neck, fingers digging into the muscles there. "Let's take a break," Redd insisted. "It's getting dark—we can look again in the morning."

I resisted. "No! We can't leave the dragon in the forest alone! It's just a baby! It doesn't even have a name yet!" I was horrified just thinking about it. Violent creatures lurked in the depths of the Greenwood Forest. Predators that could swallow a small critter in one bite.

I was going to be sick.

"We have to. Let's meet with the others one last time, and then we'll get a fresh start tomorrow. It'll be okay. It has survived hundreds of years trapped in a tiny shell. Surely it can survive one night of freedom."

My throat tightened and the backs of my eyes prickled. I was *not* going to cry. Not now. Not when I didn't have something real to cry about. "Are you sure?"

He stroked my skin soothingly. "I'm sure, love. Let's go."

I sniffled. "Okay. I hope you're right."

We stepped over fallen logs and our boots crunched through dried, icy leaves as we made our way back to town. The smell of frost and sickly-sweet decaying plant matter was hardly a comfort. I kept imagining a tiny dragon, cold, all alone, curled up by itself...

"Stop thinking about it," Redd insisted. "It's going to be okay."

But I wasn't too sure.

And then, I caught a whiff of something unexpected at the edge of the forest.

Smoke.

I inhaled again to be sure.

Yep, something was on fire.

I glanced frantically at Redd. He too had his nose turned up, smelling the smoke as well. "Oh," he murmured. "That might be something."

We took off running.

I wasn't one to run when it wasn't necessary, but desperate times called for desperate measures. And this was the most desperate of times.

We sprinted toward the smell of smoke until we could see the thin wisps crawling through the forest, gray and mysterious. My thighs thrummed with the effort.

And then we found the source.

Small, barely larger than my palm, was a pile of leaves aflame on the ground. And beside them, red and wriggling, was the dragon.

I didn't think—I simply *lunged*.

Throwing my entire body forward, hands outstretched, I dove for the little winged creature.

And I was so close, too. My fingers brushed its scaly surface, nearly finding purchase, but then the dragon squealed, loud enough to nearly burst my eardrums, and let out a blast of steaming hot air directly into my face.

Reflexively, I slapped my palms to my cheeks, sure I would find my skin had melted off. Or that my blue hair would be aflame.

I heard Redd shouting and scrambling amidst my panic.

Luckily, my skin was intact. My eyebrows, though, felt a bit singed.

Much to my dismay, the dragon had escaped with Redd hot on its tail.

I laid in the dirt for long moments, feeling bad for myself while Redd flew through the forest chasing the dragon.

It was hopeless. The flying creature was impossibly fast.

But it was still here. Still in Moonvale. And that made my spirits soar.

I folded my hands together and slipped them under my cheek while I waited for Redd to return, letting the chill of the ground sink through my clothing, into my skin.

Any nearby critters had surely been scared away in the commotion, but the forest was still so alive. Leaves settled and creaked in the breeze, rays of gentle freeze season sun fought to reach the ground through sprawling, sparse branches of trees, and a bird happily chirped somewhere in the distance.

I couldn't help but smile through the turmoil of emotions.

Eventually, Redd returned, his boot crunching blades of dead grass. Air sawed in and out of his tired lungs.

I turned my head to glance at him. He looked impossibly tall from this angle. Like one of the Old Gods returned to the realm, ominous and all-powerful.

His shoulders rose and fell with his heaving inhales and exhales and sweat glimmered on his forehead. The fact that he had worn himself ragged chasing down a baby dragon made me love him impossibly more.

I grinned, flashing my fangs. "Hi."

He huffed. His hands hung limply by his sides. "Hi, little vampire."

"Did it get away?"

"I followed it all the way to the clearing by the edge of town, but then I lost it. Little menace is *fast*."

My stomach squeezed with a weird sense of pride. What a powerful little baby, outrunning full grown vampires. "But it's still here. In Moonvale."

The corner of his mouth lifted. "It's still here. We'll catch it."

We would. We would catch it. If we had to chase it to the ends of the realm, we would catch it.

Hopefully it didn't raze the town to the ground first.

Redd bent and hooked his hands under my arms, hoisting me from the ground and onto my feet. "Let's go tell the others—they'll be happy to hear that the beast is okay. And then let's get home," he murmured. "We have a long day ahead of us tomorrow. We'll need to come up with a new plan."

I slipped my fingers between his, letting him fill the spaces in my palm. "Let's."

Redd's breath ghosted over the back of my neck as we entered our cottage, sending a shiver down my spine. I barely noticed as the door shut behind us. He reached around to unclasp my cloak and trail his fingers softly over my throat, cold from the frigid outside air.

With a sigh, I tilted my head to give him more access.

He chuckled, his fingers leaving my skin to pull off my

cloak, and then his. He tossed them aside, where they landed with a soft thud on the floor.

I turned to face him.

He was so unfairly gorgeous, my mate. His dark hair was mussed from the wind, and his brown eyes gleamed with mischief. He bit his lip, fangs poking into the flesh.

I wished those fangs were poking into *me* instead.

He grinned, as though he could sense what I was thinking.

Just when I was about to step forward and wrap my arms around him, he crouched to the floor, his hands reaching for my feet.

Fingers strong and sure, he unlaced my right boot, and then my left. I stepped out of them and kicked them aside. I didn't care where they landed.

Redd settled his hands on my calves, stroking the muscle through the fabric of my trousers. His fingers dug in for a moment.

Slowly, his hands rose, over the backs of my knees, my thighs, and then over my ass. Exploring. Kneading.

Quickly, before I could even tell what was happening, he stood and grabbed me by the waist, lifting me and whirling into the kitchen, where he settled me onto the edge of the table.

Reflexively, I wrapped my legs around his waist.

I was out of patience—I needed to kiss him. With a groan, I threaded my fingers into Redd's windblown hair, yanking his face to mine.

He kissed me like a man starved.

He tasted like ice and something primal, something that heated my veins and tightened my stomach.

His lips stroked along mine, desperate, hurried, hungry. When I parted my mouth to deepen the kiss, desperate for more, he retreated, his mouth dropping to my chin, my throat. I whined.

I couldn't decide what I wanted more—for him to kiss me or bite me.

"Redd," I pleaded.

"I've got you," he murmured against the tender skin of my throat. He lingered for a moment, scraping his fangs against my jugular in a tease that made me writhe with need.

My hips churned, desperate for contact. "Please."

"Patient, Fiella. You know I'll always take care of you."

"Just bite me. One little bite," I begged. My fangs ached at the thought of the euphoria that accompanied the bite. He would drink from me, and then it would be my turn. It would be utter bliss. I salivated.

"Not yet," he said softly. He unbuttoned my blouse, slowly, letting it drop to the table behind me.

My breasts were free beneath—I didn't bother strapping them down when I was wearing thick clothing and cloaks anyway.

He dragged his mouth from my throat, over my sternum. His hands settled onto my ribs.

Redd's callused thumbs stroked the undersides of my breasts until I was squirming. Panting. When I was prepared to beg once again, he turned his face, capturing one of my nipples in his mouth.

I groaned, my head dropping back. I buried my hands in his hair, clutching him to me.

"Yes," I hissed. "Bite me."

He chuckled, but he did as I asked, lightly nipping at my sensitive flesh. The sting was delicious, traveling down my spine and pooling in my center. My heart thumped heavily in my chest.

It wasn't enough to draw blood, much to my dismay.

He teased my taut nipple with his tongue, drawing a quiet moan from my throat.

I allowed my hands to settle onto his shoulders, my fingernails digging into the fabric of his tunic. When I tried to tug on his tunic, to pull it off, he dipped out of my grasp, dropping to his knees on the floor in front of me. He glanced up to meet my gaze.

The sight of him on his knees before me was enough to destroy me completely.

He grinned, his fangs glinting.

And then he hooked his long fingers into the waistband of my trousers. He tugged on the fabric. "Lift," he commanded.

"You don't have to; it's been a long day—"

"Lift. Or I'll tear them off."

The look in his eye told me he wasn't bluffing. Obediently, I braced my hands behind me, lifting my ass from the table. He yanked my trousers and undergarments off in one smooth motion, leaving me completely bare.

He shoved my knees apart, as wide as they would go.

I was spread out obscenely on the table in front of him, and he looked at me like a treat he wanted to devour.

He licked his lips. "Gods, woman. You have no idea how much of my day I spend craving the taste of you."

Before I could formulate a coherent response, he dipped his head, swiping his tongue over my pussy.

I groaned. My fingers fisted in his hair, desperate for something to hold onto.

He didn't hold back.

He feasted on me, unrestrained, scraping my tender flesh with his fangs and drawing hoarse cries from my throat. His tongue teased my clit in a rhythm he had perfected that was sure to send me hurtling over the edge.

He knew my body better than I thought possible—every inch of me bowed to his command.

When he slid two fingers into my core, fucking me slowly, I shattered.

Lights danced in my vision as my body convulsed. I screamed, the sound garbled and strained, but I could hardly hear it through the ringing in my ears. The orgasm tore through me, fast and hot, leaving me breathless.

When my lungs could draw air again, I released the punishing grasp on Redd's hair, allowing him to stand to his full height and lift me from the table.

And when Redd tossed me onto the bed, slowly unbuttoning his trousers and letting them drop to the floor, I knew we wouldn't be getting any sleep after all.

# CHAPTER 5

# *Kizzi*

Hex pounded against the window with a fury that would've been impressive if it wasn't so fucking annoying.

Night had fallen, and along with it came a frosty chill that permeated all the way to the bone.

I did *not* want to open the damned window. But I didn't really have a choice.

"Why do you want the window opened, Hex? It's freezing. And you don't like the cold, remember? It makes you stiff."

Hex merely pounded harder. If I wasn't careful, they were sure to break through my protection enchantment and shatter the glass pane.

I sighed heavily, letting the air rush past my clenched teeth. "Fine. But just for a moment. And then we're going to sleep, we've got a big day tomorrow."

The window's latch bit into my fingers with an uncomfortable chill. I really needed to bulk up on firewood or remind Tandor to do it for me. One of the perks of having an orc as a partner—they did all the heavy lifting for you, even when you didn't ask.

It was wonderful.

Tandor was, much to my jealousy, curled up in bed at his own cottage, probably peacefully sleeping by now. He had an early morning at Ginger's Pub, and I had some locating potions that I needed to finish before the two suns rose in the morning.

We were both exhausted after long hours trudging through the forest.

I was determined to track down that dragon, no matter what it took.

My cauldron bubbled quietly, infusing the potion with magic and boiling it into a smooth liquid.

Since the return of the magic on Hallow's Eve, spells and enchantments came readily. Easily. With minimal effort. It felt as though the well of magic inside of me was limitless. I didn't push it, though. The coven, and especially Ani, had warned me against it.

I wasn't positive if I was the reason the magic had returned, but I couldn't exactly rule it out, either.

It felt impossible. Ridiculous. But Ani insisted.

And I did have that weird dream during the ritual...

Whatever. I brushed the thought away. There were more urgent things to worry about.

When the window eased open and a blast of frigid wind brushed my hair back from my face, Hex tensed, coiled, and then sprang through the window. I reached for them, but I was too slow.

"Hex!" I screamed. "Don't! It's dark!" Panic tightened my chest and clawed its way up my throat.

Hex wasn't always by my side, but they were always close. Always nearby. And as they disappeared into the darkness, I couldn't resist the urge to follow them.

But it was fucking *freezing*.

Grumbling and cursing my familiar the entire time, I donned my boots and slipped my warmest cloak over my nightclothes.

I lit an enchanted lantern and followed Hex into the night.

"Hex!" I hissed, mindful of the volume of my voice so I wouldn't wake any sleeping folk. I could sense Hex's nearness, could almost smell them, but I still couldn't see them.

They had led me to the stables at the end of town. What Hex needed in the stables in the dead of night was beyond me. But I followed them anyway.

"Hex, I swear to the Old Gods, let's go home or I'll—I'll —" I struggled to come up with an adequate threat. I had already threatened to smear them on the cobblestones. I couldn't maim them, nor did they have any possessions I could take away. "I'll refuse to remove any pieces of lint from you for weeks!"

My heart rate quickened in my chest. Yes, that had certainly horrified them.

The lantern cast an eerie orange glow around me, bringing the stables into view. A few horses stared at me with wide, glossy eyes, certainly curious about why they were being disturbed. I patted one on the neck as I passed.

It was a gorgeous black stallion. Nightmare. I was surprised to find him still in Moonvale. I ran my fingers through his mane. "Hello, old friend," I murmured as I stepped around to the back of the structure.

Finally, my lantern light gleamed on something purple and shiny. Hex.

"Hex!" I hissed. "What in Hell's Realm are you doing?"

They were curled up on a pile of hay, which was surprising, considering hay was one of the textures they usually avoided. I approached slowly. They wouldn't attack me. I was pretty sure.

Well, they did attack me sometimes, but I provoked them so that was my own fault.

I reached out with cold, shaking fingers. "Hey, buddy. Let's go home."

When my fingers met Hex's slippery surface, they softened and slipped aside.

I slapped a hand over my mouth to trap the scream that threatened to escape.

There, in the hay, sleeping peacefully under Hex, was the baby dragon.

My heart thundered in my chest. I worried that it was so loud, it would wake the slumbering beast.

For a few moments, I allowed myself to panic. Fear and relief warred for control over my mind.

The dragon was here. The dragon was *here*.

And I didn't know what the fuck to do with it now.

Could I just... scoop it up? Carry it like a cat? Casper

didn't like it when I carried her. Actually, none of the cats in town really let folk scoop them up if they could help it.

I couldn't leave it here, that was certain. The stables were warmer than the open forest, with the bodies of the horses radiating heat, but it was still uncomfortably chilly.

And the dragon was just a baby!

I leaned in to get a closer look while I formulated my plan.

They were tiny—somewhere between a squirrel and a cat in size. Their skin was a rich red color that shimmered beautifully under the glow of my lantern. Four thin legs with knobby knees were curled beneath a small oval body that rose and fell with smooth breaths. I couldn't see the feet to be able to see if there were any claws, but I assumed there were.

A ridge of spines traveled from the dragon's brow, over their neck, and down their back, thickening directly between their ears. Small, stumpy horns dotted the top of the creature's head. A spindly tail flicked lazily in dreamy motion.

I glanced at Hex for help. "Okay, familiar. I know we don't usually work in a dynamic like this, but right now, I'm laying down the law. Do what familiars do and help me. Please."

Hex stubbornly ignored me. I forced down the urge to curse at them.

I cleared my throat, trying a different approach—bribery. Bribery worked on everyone, even magical slime creatures. "Fine. I'll let you sleep at the foot of my bed for one whole night. And I won't even complain about it."

They perked up. I was close.

"Two nights."

Closer. They inched away from the dragon.

Tandor was going to kill me.

"One week. Final offer."

With a bolt of joy, Hex wrapped themself around my ankle for a moment before they returned to the dragon, slipping beneath them and creating a strange sort of slime cradle.

It was only a little horrifying, the way they were able to pick the critter up.

Hex's power was still a mystery that I chose not to examine too closely.

"Oh, yes, that's great! Easy, now. Don't wake them."

We inched toward my apothecary, Hex slipping over the ground like a ghost and me following, lantern clutched in white-knuckled fingers.

I prayed that nobody would witness this spectacle.

The town was still getting used to Hex. I didn't want to terrify everyone with this display.

I resorted to flattery.

"Hey, Hex, you're doing a great job. Keep going, sweetie!"

Hex turned and spat at me.

"Right. Not sweetie. Sorry." I picked up my pace. "You're the most impressive and scary familiar in the entire realm."

That worked. Hex expanded and moved even faster. I had to jog to keep up.

Without incident, thank the fates, we made it back to my shop without the dragon waking, or any folk running into us.

Once we were inside, though, I was stumped once again.

Again, I wished Tandor was here. He was always better at brainstorming than I was.

I briefly considered waking him up, or Fiella and Redd, but they needed the sleep after running through the town all evening.

And I was supposedly the Hand of the Dragons. I could handle this.

Maybe.

I hadn't even considered what I would do with the dragons if they ever hatched. Or where I would keep them. Or how I would stop the shop from burning down if they could actually breathe fire like they did in legends and storybooks.

"Okay, Hex. We can do this. You keep the dragon asleep and comfortable, and I'll do... something. I'll mix up a protection charm and strengthen my door and window enchantments. I don't want to chase this one through the forest again."

Hex promptly carried the dragon over to my bed, where they settled in on top of my pillows.

I should have expected that.

I sighed. At least they looked like they wouldn't be moving for a while. Just to be sure, I dusted some sleep-inducing powder over the dragon, enough to keep it docile and dreaming for a few hours.

I got to work.

I packed up my incomplete Merry Day gifts to make room on my worktable. And then I gathered my ingredients.

The sprites were surprisingly helpful, now that they could speak to me in their weirdly admiring way. They still screwed things up by trying to be overly helpful, rearranging shelves on a whim, but since I knew they could understand my vague threats now, they were more effective. Sometimes.

"Hey, Scarlett! Where did I leave the willow bark? Don't touch it, I don't want it to burn, but I can't remember for the life of me where I tucked it."

"It's in the bottle on the top shelf, Godsblood."

"It's Kizzi," I reminded. "Thank you." The bottle was corked and pushed to the back of the shelf, and I needed a stool to reach it. It would have taken me forever to find without the sprite's help.

I smiled to myself.

Even if they moved my ingredients, at least they could now tell me where they were.

It was almost like having my own personal flock of tiny magical employees.

After many trips back and forth, my table was full. Tree bark, insect wings, plants, flowers, the trimmings from a horse hoof, three strands of my hair, and a spoonful of honey.

I grabbed a small cauldron and got to work.

This mixture would boil down into a fine powder that could be dusted on doors and windows to strengthen any existing enchantments. In my case, I needed to bump up my protection spells. To keep thieves and wrong doers out, sure, but also to keep precious critters in.

I set the brew to boiling. With a little magical encouragement, and a softly hummed chant, it would boil down in minutes rather than hours.

The smell wafting off the cauldron was nowhere close to pleasant. Actually, it was fucking gross, but it was a necessary side effect of the process. And there was no way I would be opening the window—I was still defrosting from my trip to the stables.

I grabbed a book from my shelf and sat down to read to pass the time.

Casper, the fluffy white cat that I hadn't seen enter, jumped onto my lap and curled up comfortably. I didn't try to pet her; she didn't always let me, and I didn't want to make her leave.

I liked her company. I was a full-blown softie.

A sprite settled onto my shoulder, probably reading the book alongside me. I hoped they liked werewolf smut. I had the urge to shield their eyes from any unsavory bits, but they could make their own decisions and would flee if they felt the words were too scandalous.

It almost felt like a book club. Fiella appreciated my taste in literature, but not everyone did. And she was much more outspoken about it than I was, too. I kept my novels tucked safely away from prying eyes to avoid any judgement.

Fiella would talk about them in a crowded pub if nobody stopped her. The vampire had no shame.

When the scent turned from acrid to smokey, I set the book aside and returned to the cauldron. The contents were charred and blackened, reduced to a chunky ash mixture. Perfect. I grabbed a pestle and ground the chunks into a fine powder.

As I worked, I hummed the enchantment under my breath. I glanced nervously at my bed to make sure the dragon was still sleeping to find that Hex had literally tucked them into my covers.

I really needed to figure out a name for the dragon at some point. It was getting old thinking about them as just "the dragon". Maybe they would appreciate something pretty, like Rose. Or Daffodil. Or if they would be particular like Hex and demand to choose their own name.

The other two eggs were, gratefully or unfortunately, still sitting unchanged in the cracked cauldron. It was probably for the best—if they all had hatched at the same time we would really be in trouble.

Scooping the powder concoction into the palm of my hand, I quickly performed a ritual on the door and windows, securing the building. I could've sworn I heard echoes of the chant from the sprites in the shop, but that must have been my imagination.

Magic hummed in the air, lifting loose strands of my hair and buzzing my bones. I breathed it in deep, relishing the way it filled my lungs and fizzled through my veins.

As it faded, a wave of exhaustion took over.

The suns were close to rising, I would get scarce few hours of sleep by the look of things.

I didn't even have the energy to remove the dragon from my bed. I crawled under the covers, staying on the very edge of the bed to keep a wide gap between the critter and me. It was impossibly warm, radiating heat more than even Tandor did.

I resisted the urge to snuggle up to them. I didn't think they would appreciate it, and I wasn't in the mood to get bit by those sharp little teeth.

I looked around for a flash of white fur. Casper might as well pile into the bed, too, while we were at it. As if she read my mind, the small cat hopped onto the foot of the bed and promptly curled up and closed her eyes.

It was a gods damned slumber party all over again.

Tandor would lose his mind if he could see this right now.

Feeling strangely comfortable and exhausted to the bone, while tiny movements jostled strands of my hair, sleep pulled me under.

# CHAPTER 6

# Fiella

"Do you think she's dead?" I asked Redd, pounding my fist into the front door of Kizzi's apothecary shop for what felt like the thousandth time.

"She's not dead," he murmured. "Probably still sleeping. Or out searching early."

"Kizzi doesn't wake up early," I grumbled. She barely woke up earlier than I did, and that wasn't saying much. I pounded on the door harder. "Kizziah Cedarton!"

"Don't you have a key?" Redd asked calmly, oblivious to the seed of panic that was blooming in the pit of my stomach.

"Not anymore."

"You lost it?"

I glanced at him sidelong. "Maybe."

He exhaled through his nose. "She's somewhere."

"Very helpful," I snapped. "Thanks."

He lifted his brows at me, turning to examine the door. He peered at the wood, fresh and bright, repaired only weeks ago by himself. He ran his fingers over the hinges, squinting in concentration. "Should I get my tools and take the door off?"

Finally, a helpful idea. "Yes! Yes. Let's do that. I'll wait here in case she shows up."

Redd planted a quick, firm kiss on my forehead before he hurried in the direction of his new woodworking shop, his strides long and fast.

I kept knocking. And shouting. If I wasn't careful, I'd start to draw a crowd.

I didn't care.

"Kizzi!" I shouted again, dragging her name out like I was belting a song. "Open up or my mate will take the door down!"

Still nothing.

I kept knocking.

I had already tried the windows, shoving my fingers in the crevices in an attempt to force my way through, but they were as solid as steel. I doubted even throwing a boulder at the glass would make a scratch.

The tender skin on the side of my hand bloomed into shades of red and brown, swelling angrily.

Eventually, Redd returned, tools in hand and determination clenching the muscles of his jaw.

He got to work.

He hammered, sawed, even pried with a crowbar.

It made no difference. His forehead gleamed with sweat from the effort, and the door did not budge.

Tears threatened to squeeze my throat and prick the backs of my eyes.

"Kizzi, this isn't funny! Open up!"

Miraculously, as I was manhandling the doorknob in

another attempt to break it, the knob turned.

The door swung open.

Kizzi stood there, scrubbing a fist over tired eyes, her hair a wild mass of green tangles and a cloak hastily tugged around her shoulders. "Gods!" she groaned. "Why do you look like that? Who died?"

I shoved my way inside. "You did! We've been knocking for hours!"

Redd followed behind me, pulling the door shut with a loud click that raised the hairs on my arms. A slimy sensation slithered over my skin. I shivered. *Magic.*

"You knocked? I didn't hear a thing. Did you at least bring tea?"

My jaw dropped open in outrage. "Did I bring tea? I was trying to rescue you from death's door!"

"I just woke up a minute ago. I'm perfectly fine."

"Did you miss the part I mentioned about the knocking? For hours?"

Redd interrupted me. "A few minutes, really."

I glared at him. "Ages."

Kizzi shrugged. "I must've been in a deep sleep. Oh, I increased the protection enchantments on the door and windows, too. That could've done it."

I fought off a surge of annoyance. "You think?"

A sound from Kizzi's back bedroom snagged my attention. It was somewhere between a trill and a growl—like the purr of a cat. A large, scary cat. Sookie, my own cat baby, had sweet precious purrs. This one was... more.

Kizzi snapped into movement, suddenly looking much more awake. "Oh!"

"What's that? Hex eating rocks again?" I asked.

"Hex doesn't eat rocks," the witch said distractedly as she grabbed a cloth from a basket and headed back into her room. "They just wanted to try it that one time."

I snorted. "Sure. Whatever you say. Weirdos."

A strange smell caught my attention then. Something like ozone and fire, different from the usual magic and cinnamon scent of Kizzi's apothecary. Something wild. I tilted my head, glancing at Redd to see if he noticed it too. He was too busy tracking a sprite with his eyes, watching him attempt to flip through the pages of a book that was much bigger than he was.

Kizzi fumbled noisily with something in her room, huffing with effort. Grumbled curses mixed with the sound of rustling fabric.

"Kiz?" I asked. "What's going on in there? Is Tandor here?" I shivered with that thought, imagining the horror of interrupting my best friend and her man doing something unsavory. "You have guests over!"

"Oof," she huffed. "One second! You're going to love this."

"Am I?" I braced myself for something horrifying. Like garlic. Or disgusting. Like bugs. Or somewhere in between. There were countless unpleasant possibilities.

"I would've shown you earlier, but... I've been a little busy fortifying the place."

"Okay. Now I'm nervous."

She cursed again. Smoke met my nostrils. Had she blown out a candle? "Almost. Ready. Hang on."

I crossed my arms, leaning my hip against a shelf. I couldn't see much through the doorway to Kizzi's back bedroom, as she had kicked it most of the way shut.

My stomach snarled, echoed by a slight twinge in my throat. I needed a pastry as soon as possible or I would surely perish.

My thirst for blood had been almost entirely quenched as of late, thanks to my wonderful mate and his eager willingness to share the blood pumping through his veins. My cheeks warmed at the thought of his fangs in my flesh, and mine in his. The euphoria that accompanied. I glanced in his direction to meet his gaze, and he lifted a brow at my expression.

We were interrupted by Kizzi kicking the door to her bedroom open wide. It met the far wall with a smack that rattled glass bottles on shelves.

My jaw hit the floor. Redd inhaled sharply.

There, curled in Kizzi's arms, wrangled into a chaotic bundle of cloth, was the little dragon, looking drowsy and furious. Fire sparked in its eyes.

"Surprise!" Kizzi said quietly. Her expression was tense, her cheeks flushed, and her jaw clenched tight. A strand of her green hair hanging by her ear was charred and curled in on itself. Burned.

I couldn't tell if she was happy or scared. Or both.

"You found him."

"I did. Well, technically, Hex did. I gave him a sleeping potion, but I think it's wearing off. Wait, how do you know it's a boy?"

I shrugged. I couldn't put a finger on it, really. I just knew. Something about the way the scales flared over the creature's forehead. "I think his name is Ember."

"You think?"

I shrugged again, feeling confused and helpless. "I think. You're the one with the magic. You tell me."

Kizzi stepped closer, holding the wriggling mass in her arms as tightly as she could. "I've been trying to figure out the name, but nothing came to me. The fates must've wanted you to know."

That sentiment warmed my stomach. I felt special. Chosen. Sure, Kizzi was the Hand of the Dragons or whatever, but I wasn't useless.

I peered at the creature, meeting his burning gaze. He didn't look evil, he looked more nervous than anything. I would be, too, if I was a baby thrust into a scary, new world after living in a cozy eggshell for hundreds of years.

"Hi, Ember," I said to the dragon, feeling only a little stupid. There was no way the creature would understand me, but I didn't know how else to forge a connection.

The dragon huffed, letting out a small wisp of steam between sharp teeth. They looked even sharper than my own fangs. Impressive. I was a little jealous.

Kizzi shifted onto her heels. "What do we do with him?"

I considered this. "Well, we definitely don't want him to run away again."

"Naturally."

"But it feels mean to keep him cooped up, too."

She sighed. "I thought the same thing. I can let him roam the shop, but that's not much."

"Do you think we can... train him?"

She examined the dragon, adjusting her grip to get a better look. "That's actually not a bad idea. It wouldn't hurt to try." The dragon exhaled again, this time letting the steaming air drift past Kizzi's exposed fingers. She flinched. "Maybe I should make us some fireproof gear."

"Yes. Let's do that. And food. What do dragons eat?"

"We should've prepared for this."

Redd snorted out a laugh. "Probably. Let's see if we can track down any more books on dragon lore. In the meantime, we'll just give him some options and see what he likes."

"And some pastries for us, too," I added. "I'm starving."

"You're always starving," Kizzi muttered, at the same time Redd said, "Of course, love."

"Has Ember just been in here for hours, then?" I asked. "Tell me everything."

"He's been sleeping. Hex helped me get him back here, and then they both curled up and passed out. I blew some sleeping dust into his face to be sure he stayed asleep. He didn't start to wake up until you got here."

"Try setting him down. What's the worst that could happen?"

"Well," Redd started. "He could burn the place down, or shred us all to pieces—"

"I didn't actually want answers. Just do it. You'll have to let him free eventually."

Kizzi donned a worried expression. "I wish Tandor was here, so we would have four folk. Four against one, those are better odds. Plus Hex. And the sprites. I think we can handle him."

Kizzi was interrupted by the door swinging open. "Talking about me, little witch?" the green orc said with a bright grin. The room felt more crowded when he entered, his brawn taking up a lot of space.

The tension in the witch's muscles loosened. "Your timing is impressive." She glanced pointedly at the squirming bundle in her arms. "We got him. And now we're going to let him go and see what happens."

Tandor, to his credit, kept his composure. He merely pushed the door shut, turned the lock, and planted his feet, looking more like a bodyguard than a pub orc. "Sure, Kiz. I'm ready."

"Let's do this!" I shouted. Nerves and anticipation fluttered in my stomach.

Redd drifted to my side, looking like he might throw his body in front of mine if he had to. He nodded in Kizzi's direction. "We'll be fine," he assured.

Kizzi held her breath for a moment before letting it out in a rush. "Okay. Okay. We're doing this."

"We're doing this," I agreed.

"I'm going to let the baby dragon go. Even though he was extremely hard to catch."

"You are," I urged.

"And it's going to be fine."

"Set the dragon down, Kiz. Quit stalling."

She smiled bashfully. "You're right. Okay. Three, two..." She crouched, setting Ember on the floor and gently unwrapping the cloth from around the dragon's body.

Adrenaline tightened my muscles, sped my pulse, brought my senses into sharp focus. I was ready for anything.

At first, nothing happened.

We all stared at the dragon as it sat on the floor, looking around curiously.

"Well," Tandor mused. "That was anticlimactic."

"Don't jinx us," Kizzi said.

Ember slowly rose onto unsteady legs, looking more like a baby deer than a fearsome beast of legend. His wings unfurled and stretched. The veins were visible through the thin skin, dark and faintly pulsing.

We all tensed, prepared for the dragon to take flight, but he didn't. He simply curled his wings back up and then took an unsteady step. And then another, more solid. And another. With a start, I realized he was walking toward me.

I froze, holding perfectly still, not sure if I wanted to scream and jump up and down or throw up and cry.

My pulse hammered erratically in my chest.

Redd rested a reassuring hand on my shoulder, warm and solid.

The dragon approached, slowly, timidly, sniffing the air the entire time.

I held my breath.

And then the dragon stretched open its tiny maw.

# CHAPTER 7

## Kizzi

Fiella trembled like a leaf. It would have been hilarious if I wasn't also terrified and on the verge of vomiting myself.

She watched the dragon warily, as if it was capable of swallowing her whole. Redd, to my surprise, didn't pull her from the dragon's path. He simply watched the dragon with the sharp gaze of a predator, prepared to step in and protect his mate if he needed to, but willing to let her have this moment on her own.

I admired him for that. I knew the protective instincts were hard to quell.

When Ember opened his jaws and tensed, I expected a stream of unholy flames. For all of us to die and burn to a crisp, and for the shop to crumble to ash.

I tensed to leap. At what, I wasn't sure. I certainly wasn't fireproof, but if Fiella was going to burn, I was going to burn with her.

It was futile.

All that escaped the mouth of the tiny dragon was a puny

squeak, followed by a burst of hot air that merely fluttered Fiella's cloak.

I let out the heaviest exhale. My head swam with relief.

The room settled into a tense silence, all of us brushing off the near-death experience. I wiped a bead of sweat off of my forehead. The dragon closed his maw and stared at Fiella questioningly.

"Well," Tandor said awkwardly. "That was kind of adorable."

Fiella choked. "Adorable! I almost died!"

Redd rubbed her shoulder. "You were very brave."

She hadn't been brave at all, actually. She screamed like a wailing baby. But I wasn't going to say that out loud, because I had let out a squeal or two myself.

"I'm going to try something..." Tandor stepped forward slowly, extending his hand. His fingers trembled.

I should've known the gentle orc would be the first to attempt to pet the murderous creature. I couldn't decide if I wanted to smile or shove him out of the way to protect him. The indecision kept me rooted to the spot.

He knelt, slowly, hesitantly. His muscles twitched with the restraint—I could tell he was itching to scoop the tiny dragon up in one smooth motion.

The dragon glanced in his direction and tilted his head curiously, and then turned back to face Fiella.

The tension in the room was begging to be shattered. Even the sprites seemed to hold their breath.

My fingertips buzzed with restrained magic. It pressed on my fingernails, tightened my veins until it was almost painful. I curled my fingers into my palms to relieve the sensation.

Tandor's eyebrow furrowed in concentration. After what

felt like ages, his fingers finally made contact with the tiny dragon, stroking feather lightly down the middle of the creature's back.

The dragon tensed for a moment, bared its razor-sharp teeth. His scales rose like hackles. And then he laid down, allowing Tandor to pet him for a few long moments.

"Kizzi," Tandor whispered. "Are you seeing this?"

"I see it," I whispered back. "Are you scared?"

"Shitless."

"Is he soft?"

"No, it's like tiny, paper-thin stones laying on top of each other."

"No way."

He nodded encouragingly. "Come feel."

I had held the dragon earlier, but that had been more like wrangling a sleeping beast than stroking a cute critter. I looked at Fiella pointedly. "You first."

"Me?" she croaked. "No way!"

"He's looking at you. He wants you to pet him."

The dragon was actually now peering around the room. He didn't look murderous, though. If anything, he looked noble and reverent.

"Come on," I urged. "It's your dragon."

The vampire's eyes bulged. "Oh, fuck. I forgot about that part. It feels wrong—he feels too powerful."

"You better get used to him. Go on. Pet."

She steeled herself. Then, slowly, she knelt next to Tandor, who was now happily petting the dragon without a care in the world. *Silly, sweet man.*

Redd hovered close, prepared to intervene at any moment if things went south.

A tiny voice shouted from somewhere behind my shoulder. "It's going well, Godsblood!"

I jumped. I had almost forgotten about the sprites.

Fiella stifled a laugh. "Yeah, *Godsblood*."

"Shut up," I grumbled to her. To Dropp, the water sprite, I said a little louder, "Kizzi. Just Kizzi. We've been over this."

"Yes, Godsblood. I can't help it," Dropp said solemnly.

I huffed out a sigh.

It was a miracle that things hadn't gone catastrophically wrong. Somehow, Tandor and Fiella were happily (if timidly) petting the baby dragon, and all of their fingers were still attached.

The sprites were watching from perches all over the room, but none of them were brave enough to get close.

Redd's eyes were glued to the side of Fiella's face, and a small smile tugged at the corner of his usually hard mouth.

Hex, my gods damned familiar, was snoozing in the broken cauldron with the remaining two eggs.

And Casper was nowhere to be seen, which wasn't out of the norm. It was probably for the best.

I took a moment to appreciate the blessing from the fates.

And then the peaceful moment burst.

A knock pounded on the front door, muffled through the strengthened enchantments and barely audible. It was no surprise I had slept through Fiella's knocking earlier—it was barely louder than a squirrel crunching on an acorn.

Everyone froze, even Tandor, who gently grabbed Fiella's wrist and pulled her hands away from the dragon to protect her from any startle. Her reflexes should have been faster, but Fiella was Fiella.

The knock sounded again.

"Are you going to get that?" Redd asked.

It took effort to lift my feet from the ground, they wanted to stay rooted. "Right. Sure. Yes. I'm going to answer the door."

"Any time soon?" Redd prompted.

I laughed tightly. "Of course. It's just—"

"Just what?"

"I'm afraid to open the door. What if Ember runs out again?"

"We'll catch him," Redd said confidently. He glanced at Fiella and Tandor. Fiella, who shared most of his quick vampire reflexes, even though her Pa was human. And Tandor, who was big and strong enough to handle most beasts.

I was doubtful, and my face must have shown it.

"We can handle a baby dragon, princess," Tandor said. "Answer the door."

I still hadn't managed to shake the "princess" nickname. I would never admit that it was growing on me.

Before I could move, another voice called out, "I'll get it, Godsblood."

Dropp, followed by a few other sprites, flew over to the door. To my absolute astonishment, the tiny creatures worked together to push through the enchantment, disengage the lock, and pull the door open. My jaw hung wide.

Somehow, some way, the tiny sprites were strong enough to pull open a door that had to be at least a hundred times their weight. It should have been impossible.

"No fucking way," I said, shocked. "You guys can open the door?"

"Of course, Godsblood. How did you think we came and went?"

To be honest, I hadn't ever thought about it. But it did make sense. They had caused all sorts of mischief in my shop, so of course they were capable of impressive feats.

I realized they could have done real damage to my shop, if they chose to. But they never did. Even back when I couldn't communicate with them. Stupidly, my heart squeezed.

"Be ready!" I called to the room as a whole.

I had no hope of catching a dragon, even with my magic, so I simply braced myself and watched the door swing open, content to let the others save the day for once.

Ginger stood outside. "It's about time!" she shouted. Her voice was ragged and cracked. "I've been screaming out here! Didn't you hear me?"

"Sucks, doesn't it?" Fiella muttered. "Been there."

"It does! I was just—woah!" The faun yelped as the sprites grabbed onto her and yanked her into the building before slamming the door shut behind her. They pulled her by her cloak, her antlers, even locks of her auburn hair. She fluttered her hands helplessly.

The dragon bolted toward freedom, but he was too slow —the door slammed in his face.

He let out a small huff.

I let out a shuddering exhale.

The room collectively took a breath.

Ginger straightened her cloak. "Well, that was a bit violating." She furrowed her brows at the sprites, who were fluttering back to their places on the shelves. "I would've come in on my own."

"Well…" I gestured to the dragon, who was right by Ginger's ankles, staring longingly at the closed door.

Ginger jumped. Her hooves clacked when she landed, and she scurried back a few paces. She didn't know where to stand. She was stuck somewhere between wanting to approach and wanting to flee. "Fates!" she shouted. "Why didn't anyone tell me that you caught it? I've been looking all morning."

She looked around the room, a slight hurt expression pinching her eyes.

"There wasn't time," Tandor said. "We haven't been here long. It all happened so fast."

"We would've grabbed you next," Fiella added.

I nodded in agreement. We hadn't left the woman out on purpose.

"Okay…" Her eyes settled on the small red dragon. "He's pretty cute. Scary, too." She glanced at me for a moment before her gaze flitted back to Ember. "I have the strangest urge to… bow?"

"It'll pass," I agreed. "I think it's the ancient magic or something. You get used to it."

She swallowed. "Okay. That's—okay. Is it friendly? Does it have a name?"

"His name is Ember," I supplied. "And… that's to be determined. But nobody has been gravely injured yet, so that's a good sign."

"Sure! Good sign indeed." She turned to Tandor. "You pet it?"

"Sure did, boss."

She nodded. "I knew you would. And you lived to tell the tale."

"I did indeed. Not a single burn."

"Impressive."

The orc grinned. "I have a thing for critters."

Ginger snorted. "Don't we know it. I actually came looking for you. Your order of cranberries arrived."

Tandor straightened, wiping his palms on his trousers. "My cranberries! I almost forgot!" He glanced at me quickly before clearing his throat. "For... a pie. Right. That Ginger is helping me bake."

I held down a smile. Tandor had never baked a pie in his life. I knew the berries were surely for a new flavor of cider. Tandor worked at the pub with Ginger, but he was in charge of the ciders, and he loved trying new flavors.

He wasn't subtle at all, but I wasn't going to call him out on it.

"You better go take care of that," I said. "We'll be fine here."

"You sure?" He drifted over to me, placing a warm hand on the back of my neck and tugging me forward so he could plant a kiss on top of my head.

"Mhm. Go. I can handle things here. Besides, I'm sure we all have to prepare for Merry Day." I patted him on the cheek as he stepped back.

Ginger grinned. "We sure do. Let's go, Tandor. Bye, Kiz! Bye, Fiella and Redd!"

Fiella waved. "Good to see you, Ginny."

Redd nodded his head.

This time, I called out to the sprites myself. "Guys? Any help here?"

"Sure, Godsblood. Already on it." The sprites jumped into motion again, following the two folk as they departed, closing any gaps and distracting Ember enough that the door opened and closed without issue.

That was surely going to come in handy.

"Why do you look so evil over there?" Fiella said suspiciously.

I forced a blank expression onto my face. "No reason."

"Is it about the sprites that are super helpful all of a sudden?"

"It might be."

"Kiz," she reprimanded.

"I didn't even do anything!"

"But you're thinking about it."

I sighed. "I'll be nice to them, I swear." Or, nice enough.

"You better be."

I returned my attention to the dragon. "Well, what are we going to do? And what if the other two hatch? It's like taking care of a baby, but worse. Because the baby can murder folk and burn the entire town to the ground."

"Well... at least it's still a baby. It can't be too hard. Feed it, give it a comfy bed, and play with it. Maybe scratch its tiny head and kiss it on its tiny cheeks. I think we can handle that."

"So, you're taking him with you?" I asked hopefully.

"Woah, I didn't say that!"

I hurried to a basket on the table that I had prepared for this moment. I pulled out a few vials. One contained a protective enchantment similar to the one I had placed on the shop. Another contained a flame-proofing liquid. "We'll fix your cottage up, then. And then you can take him."

Redd looked pale. "Sure. Fix up the cottage. That is made almost entirely of wood."

I flapped my hand dismissively. "If it burns down, you'll

rebuild it. You're the woodworker, after all." And it was true. Since Redd had moved to Moonvale, he had opened up his own woodworking shop that was keeping him very busy. I could admit that he was adept at what he did.

He better be, considering he was my best friend's mate, and she was the most talented trinket collector in the entire realm.

He swallowed. "I guess you're right." He turned to Fiella, reaching out and running a hand down the length of her hair. "Are you sure about this?"

She leaned into his touch and smiled warmly at him. I held down the gag and rude comment that wanted to fly out of my mouth—I knew I was just as lovey dovey with Tandor.

It was absurd, how happy everyone was. It was like a gods damned fairytale.

"I'm sure," Fiella said with more conviction than I expected. "I've been waiting for this moment since I forced Kizzi to bring the eggs home."

"It's true," I added. "It really is Fiella's fault that we're in this situation in the first place."

She glared at me. "Oh hush, bitch. You wanted them just as much as I did. It's like having a murderous puppy. You'd do anything for a murderous puppy."

I simply shrugged, because I couldn't disagree. "Well," I tossed the fireproofing supplies into a bag. "Bring these home, set them up, and then I'll swing by later to strengthen up the enchantment if necessary. The sprites, Hex, and I will take care of the little monster until then."

Fiella smiled gratefully. "Of course. You really are the best, you know?"

I shoved the bag at her. "I know. Now get out, quick, while Ember is distracted."

The dragon was chasing a sprite around the room, snapping at its fluttering feet with gentle chomps.

Fiella let out a swoon, pressing her hands to her cheeks. "But he's so cute!"

I shoved her shoulder, laughing. "Go. He'll be here later."

Redd ushered her out. "Let's go, love. We still have work to do. See you, Kizzi."

"To the moons!" Fiella yelled as the door was slammed shut.

"Suns!" I called after her.

And then it was just me, the dragon, and the sprites.

Alone.

*Fuck.*

# CHAPTER 8

# Fiella

Redd and I strode through town hand in hand, munching on a new baked snack from Mitz's bakery—cookies with tiny chocolate bits in them. The sugary, sweet treat was delicious, and I had to force myself to enjoy it in small bites so I wouldn't shove the whole thing in my mouth.

My breath clouded in front of me as I spoke. "I can't believe this is happening."

"Which part?" Redd asked.

"All of it. The magic returning to the realm. Kizzi actually finding the dragon eggs. The dragon hatching. The dragon escaping. The dragon being caught again. I think I have whiplash."

Redd hummed in agreement. "Certainly never a dull moment."

"Did you think this would be your life when you came to Moonvale?"

He barked out a laugh. "Absolutely not."

Redd was from Sunhaven, a hot, crowded city on the

other side of the Barren Lands, the desolate expanse of land that separated Moonvale from the rest of the realm. Bad luck drove him to flee, and he ended up in Moonvale, where the luck followed him. It was all my fault, of course. Well, it was my ex-boyfriend's fault.

But I couldn't regret any of it, because it brought me the best man in all of the realms.

I squeezed Redd's palm. His warmth kept my fingers from freezing.

"Do you miss it?" I asked. He had been here for almost a year. At times it felt like only days since he walked into my life and into my trinket shop. But now, my life was so irrevocably entwined with his that I couldn't imagine us ever being separated.

"Miss what? Sunhaven?"

"Yeah. Home. The warmth." I gestured around me with my half-eaten cookie before taking another quick bite. "You didn't have to deal with this weather there."

"Since I laid eyes on you, Moonvale became my home. You're my home."

I leaned into his shoulder, my stomach feeling warm and fluttery. "You're just saying things."

"No, I mean it." He looked at me tenderly, his hard face softening. His facial hair was longer now, scruffy. It was soft when I ran my hands over it.

I popped the last bite of cookie into my mouth, chewed for a moment, and swallowed before speaking again. "The fates have a funny way of working, don't they?"

"Mhm," Redd agreed. He handed me the last bite of his cookie without a second thought, and I loved him all the more for it. It was even more delicious than my own cookie.

"So, what are you making for Merry Day?" I asked. Kizzi had decided that since she and Tandor had practically gone broke buying the dragon eggs, they would make gifts for each other instead of purchasing them. And that sentiment had spread.

Hence my learning to knit. It was against my will, really.

"It's a surprise."

"No fair," I whined. "You know exactly what I'm making."

"Because you keep pulling out your yarn while I'm around. And, besides, I don't know what you're making for me."

That was true. Because I honestly hadn't decided yet. I was saving his for last, in hopes that my knitting skills would be advanced by then. "I guess it'll be a surprise, too. What if I knit you a sparkly cloak? Would you wear it?"

"Er. Of course," he stammered. "If it would make you happy." His jaw clenched. I could tell the admission was painful for him, my grumpy, sullen vampire.

I laughed out loud, imagining Redd walking around wearing a monstrosity made from colorful yarn. It was enough to brighten my entire day. "I would never do that to you. Unless I was feeling particularly evil."

Redd was spared from responding when Mayor Tommins walked up to us. He was wrapped in a thick, fluffy cloak, and his mane of hair was loose, flowing in the wind. "Hello, Fiella, Redd." He nodded to each of us in turn. "I assume things are going well. The town is still standing, as far as I can tell."

"Yes! We found the little guy. Well, Kizzi did. He's accounted for."

Tommins nodded thoughtfully. "I'm glad. Now she needs to keep the beast contained."

Redd chimed in. "Well actually, boss, we'll be taking him in."

Tommins' brows rose. "Oh really? That's interesting. Interesting indeed."

I nodded. I gestured to the bag, which was slung over Redd's shoulder. "We have supplies. We're going to bulk up the protections in the cottage. Nobody will even know he's there."

The gryphon's face twisted into a strange expression for a moment before smoothing out. I couldn't tell if it was a grimace, a smile, or something else entirely. "See that you do. We don't need any more panic around town. Everyone is already on edge because of the, you know—" He gestured vaguely, obviously alluding to the mysterious return of magic to the realm.

"Of course. We've got it under control," I assured.

He nodded sharply. "Right. Well, I've got things to do, but I'll be checking in on you folk." Before he managed more than one stride in the other direction, he stopped. "Oh, wait, Redd. I think I have another job for you. Can you swing by my office this evening to discuss?"

"Sure," Redd answered. "Things are a little tight with Merry Day coming up but—"

"This will be quick," Tommins interrupted. "Easy."

Redd nodded. "Alright, then. I'll be there."

"Great. Yes. Thank you. Good day!" And with that, he strode away, his steps long and fast.

"That's mysterious," I joked, tugging Redd in the direction of the cottage we now shared on the edge of the Greenwood Forest. "What do you think he wants?"

"There's no telling. But whatever it is, it can't be any crazier than baby proofing our cottage for a dragon."

"You have a point there."

"Not there, *there*," I instructed, pointing to the windowsill in the front of the cottage. It was beside the front door and would be the second most likely exit point.

"But what about the chimney?"

"The chimney already has a protection charm on it. Remember?"

"Right, right." He moved to the windowsill, gently sprinkling a line of powder onto the wooden surface. The ingredients of the powder were a mystery that I preferred not to know the answer to. All that mattered was that it worked and kept my cottage from burning down.

After what felt like hours, we had deployed everything, setting out protective charms and enchantments to the best of our ability, following Kizzi's instructions exactly.

Magic hummed in the air and lifted the hairs on my arms, so I could only assume that it had worked.

Redd departed to meet up with Mayor Tommins, leaving me with only Sookie to keep me company while I worked on my knitting projects. The grey cat curled up on the floor beside me, glancing at me sideways when I let out particularly colorful curses.

My fingers refused to cooperate, causing knot after ugly knot in the yarn.

But I kept trying.

"You're lucky that you're a cat and will never have to knit anything," I said to Sookie as she watched me hurl the ball of yarn across the room in frustration for the second time. "It sucks."

She simply meowed in response.

# CHAPTER 9

# Kizzi

I twirled the magnifying glass in my fingers, making sure I inspected every single inch of the two remaining dragon eggs. I held the green one up higher, seeking a better angle.

There were hairline fissures, sure, but those were nothing new. They had been there since the first time I examined the scaled eggs. And a few tiny, shallow scratches that might have been a figment of my imagination.

The eggs were not going to be hatching. Not right now, at least.

And thank the Old Gods for that. One dragon was hard enough to wrangle.

My familiar was doing most of the heavy lifting. Hex, the purple sludge, was a surprisingly adequate babysitter, all things considered. They kept the dragon occupied by slithering around the room, popping bubbles, and, when necessary, physically restraining the little creature.

I refused to let myself think about how adorable it was, because it could have been a ticking time bomb. Quite literally.

Casper, fluffy as ever, curled up on my lap, her tail swishing idly back and forth. I couldn't tell if she was entertained by the baby dragon or irritated by it. Probably both.

"What are we going to do with these monsters, Casper?" I asked as I set the egg back onto the counter. "They're taking over."

Casper meowed quietly in response.

"I know right. It's madness."

I had spent my morning finishing up the Merry Day gifts for my friends and trying my best to keep Ember entertained.

I was *tired*. I ached for a nap, a cup of hot tea, and a warm pastry.

Like my wishes had manifested themselves, a muffled knock sounded on the door.

"Oh! Sorry, my friend." I nudged Casper onto the floor, where she scurried away, looking disgruntled. "Coming!" I called to the door, unsure if anyone could actually hear me through the protection enchantments.

As quickly as I could, making sure to glance over my shoulder to glare pointedly at Ember so the sprites would keep him in check, I tugged the door open.

Tandor, looking as bright and handsome as ever, quickly scurried inside, letting in a small burst of frigid air. "Delivery," he said warmly.

He clutched a sack in one hand, and two mugs in the other. The scent of ice, warm pumpkin, and berry tea drifted in beside him. It was almost as comforting as Tandor's clean rain scent. I inhaled greedily. "Hi."

"Hi, little witch. I've come with gifts. Green tea with blueberry and Mitz's fresh pumpkin muffins."

I happily snatched the sack from his hand while he set the mugs aside. "Pumpkin, my favorite."

He grinned. "I know."

Tandor slipped his arm around my waist, tucking my head under his chin and squeezing his body to mine. I let the sack of pastries drop to the table and wrapped my arms around his middle, squishing my face into his chest. "I love you," I muttered, the words muffled against the fabric of his cloak. "You always know exactly what I need."

"As I love you, my beautiful, dragon-wrangling witch."

"Did you finish your Merry Day gifts?" I asked.

"I did. Now it's just a waiting game."

"I wonder what it is," I joked.

He squeezed me. "Don't ruin the surprise."

Ember approached, timidly butting his head against Tandor's ankle. He flinched, pulling me with him as he jumped. "Oh! Hi, small dragon!"

"He has a name," I reminded.

"I know he has a name."

"Just saying."

"Has he just been hanging out here?"

I stepped away to get a better look at the small creature. "He sure has. And the place is still standing." I was strangely proud of the little dragon. It was a pretty low bar to praise the creature for not causing catastrophe but... wins were wins.

"You are the Hand of the Dragons, after all. It makes sense."

"Arbitrary title," I grumbled.

"You underestimate yourself."

"I do not. I think very highly of myself, thank you very much."

He planted a kiss on top of my head. "Of course, princess. I'm just saying. You're incredibly powerful. You're capable of bringing inanimate objects to life—a dragon would surely sense that power."

My cheeks warmed but I brushed him off. "Whatever. I think he's just tired from chasing around sprites all morning. Fiella and Redd should be about ready. Think you can wrangle the monster into a secure enough grip to transport over there?"

Tandor considered the small beast. "I should be able to manage that."

I glanced around the room. "Sprites? Think you can help us?" I peered into the broken cauldron, too. "Hex? We're going to need the whole team to help with this one."

"Of course, Godsblood. Whatever you need."

I sighed through my nose. It seemed the name would be sticking. "Thank you."

This should be easy enough.

The short trip to Fiella's was an absolute nightmare.

Ember had kicked and squirmed and spat hot air and sparks like his little life depended on it. He *really* wanted to explore the town again.

Not on our watch.

Tandor, fates bless him, was quaking with the effort of containing the small beast. His sleeves were singed, his face was flushed, and I could hardly even see him through the swarm of sprites perched all over him, trying to help.

And Hex, too, was curled up in his grasp, trying to squash the dragon into submission.

It was a rough journey.

After what felt like hours, and after several close calls, we finally arrived at Fiella and Redd's cottage on the edge of the Greenwood Forest.

I pounded on the door. "Open up, vampires! We've got a special delivery!"

The door opened just a crack. Fiella's honey-gold eye was hardly visible. "Oh! Kiz! I didn't expect you."

I shoved on the door, trying to ram her out of the way. "Yes, you did."

"I must have forgotten! It's really not a good time, why don't you come back later—"

"I know what you're doing. Quit stalling." I pushed on the door harder, but my witch strength was no match for her vampire muscles.

I could hear the timbre of Redd's voice from somewhere inside, but I couldn't make out his words. Whatever he said must have worked, though, because Fiella let out a deep, heaving sigh and finally stepped out of the way.

We flowed inside like a river breaking through a dam. First me, and then Tandor and his swarm of sprites. The door slammed shut behind us.

Fiella and Redd stood in the kitchen, both of them looking pale and nervous in the dim lantern light. The curtains were drawn, and I could feel protective magic humming in the air. Miraculously, it seemed they had set the enchantments up correctly.

Fiella gulped audibly. She twisted her fingers into her blouse. "You brought Ember."

"We did," Tandor grunted out. "He put up quite a fight. Have fun."

Fiella tilted her head. "Have fun? Wait! We're not ready—"

But it was too late, because Tandor had already knelt to the ground and released the wriggling bundle onto the floor. The sprites went too, leaping from Tandor's arms and shoulders and spreading throughout the room. There were more than I had seen in a while—hundreds, I guessed.

Many of the tiny folk surrounded the dragon, while a few others settled around the cottage, taking up protective stances.

Hex, too, followed Ember across the floor, heading to the back of the cottage.

I felt a twinge of disappointment that Hex had chosen to follow Ember instead of sticking with me. It seemed they were finally following my orders.

I couldn't decide if I was offended or proud.

I looked at Tandor quickly, raising my eyebrows in a silent question.

He pursed his lips. Shrugged.

"Good luck!" I shouted.

And then we bolted out the door, leaving Fiella and Redd to deal with the situation.

Giggling, ignoring the panicked shouts of the vampires behind us, we ran back to my shop.

They would be fine. With the sprites and Hex there to help, they didn't need us.

We had a moment of respite.

"How much time do you think we have before they come back?" Tandor asked huskily as he yanked the cloak from his shoulders and tossed it aside.

The shop was blessedly empty. Not a single sprite, familiar, or cat remained.

I loved the shop when it was crowded, but sometimes we just needed our alone time.

I yanked at the laces on my boots and tugged them off one by one. "Enough time. At least an hour."

Tandor swept an arm behind my knees, knocking me off my feet and hoisting me up to his chest in a cradle hold. I squealed in surprise.

"An hour? I think we need the whole night."

I laughed, waving a hand in the air to check the protective enchantments. They felt secure. "I could lock the place up, just for one night."

He grinned wickedly. "Do that. I've missed you, little witch. You've been too busy for me lately."

"I'm never too busy for you," I murmured. The air huffed out of my lungs when Tandor tossed me onto the bed, knocking fluffy pillows onto the floor.

He crawled over me, his knees on either side of my hips and his hands planted above my head.

He looked so big from this angle—completely surrounding me.

I slipped my hands around the back of his neck, trying to pull his mouth down to mine.

He resisted, chuckling. "Want something?"

I pouted. "Kiss me."

He dipped, quickly pressing his lips to my forehead before pulling away from me again. His grin was so broad, his small lower tusks were visible in the lantern light.

He was so beautiful. From his full lips, his eyes so dark they could swallow me whole, to the silky black hair that flopped over his forehead, I could stare at him all day.

I feasted on him with my eyes.

I still couldn't believe that this orc was mine. *Mine.*

"Fine, when you look at me like *that*, I can't resist," he growled.

Finally, he dipped his head and pressed his lips to mine. I sighed against his mouth.

His lips were warm, and comfortable, and perfect. I could drown in them if he let me.

His tongue stroked along my bottom lip, and I opened my mouth, granting him entry, desperate for whatever he was willing to give me. My blood burned with desire.

Tandor's tongue danced with mine, melting me, turning my body molten. I craved more. I craved *everything*.

I dropped my hand between our bodies, allowing my fingers to slip into his trousers and dance over his cock. He was so hard; he was practically throbbing. His skin was hot to the touch and deliciously smooth, a sharp contrast to the ring that pierced the tip, that was almost cold in comparison. I circled his cock with my fingers, stroking him as far as I could reach from the restrictive angle.

He groaned and grabbed my wrist to halt my movements. "Slow down," he pleaded.

I shook my head, meeting his gaze. His dark eyes bored

into mine. Ensnared me. "I don't want to wait anymore," I said quietly. "I want you inside me. Now."

He shuddered, breaking my gaze to drop his head down to my neck. "That mouth of yours is going to be the death of me," he mumbled against the skin of my throat, but he released his hold on my wrist only long enough to yank his cock free and shove my skirts out of the way.

He didn't even bother to remove our clothes—I knew he was as desperate as I was.

His cock teased at my entrance, the piercing cool against my wet, flushed skin. I hooked my legs around his waist and dug in my heels, urging him forward. "Please," I begged.

He obliged, sinking into me in one fluid motion. We both groaned at the sensation. He filled me so thoroughly, so completely, that my body almost couldn't handle it.

It was a delicious agony.

As he moved, fucking me in a fast, desperate rhythm, I clung to him, unable to do anything but hang on.

He fisted my hair and tilted my head back so he could devour my mouth in a frantic kiss as well, our lips clashing, our tongues tasting.

The orgasm was swift and brutal, building in my stomach and tearing through me before I could even scream Tandor's name. My body shuddered, my mouth dropping open into a silent shout as my core clenched around Tandor's length, milking him.

He found his release immediately, a strangled shout escaping his throat as his rhythm faltered, his pumping hips struggling to keep moving through his bliss.

When the waves of pleasure released me, I laughed at the

situation, at how Tandor and I were both disheveled, flushed, and still fully clothed.

The second time we came together, we made sure to remove our clothing first.

Later, as we laid sweaty and tangled in each other, a distinct sound rang from the front room.

*Crack. Pop. Pop.*

Tandor and I sat up immediately.

"*Fuck.*"

# CHAPTER 10

# Fiella

I was going to kill Kizzi.

Not actually, of course. But spiritually, I wanted to flay the bitch.

I needed a cider. Or five.

"Not up there! Get down!" I shouted for what felt like the hundredth time. Ember was now perched on top of my highest shelf, nestled between a delicate glass bowl and a few ancient scrolls.

Things the dragon could destroy in an instant.

Ember simply swished his tail, making direct eye contact. Stubborn little shit.

"At least don't breathe on the scrolls. They're *very* flammable."

"I don't think he knows what flammable means," Redd said gently.

I glared at him.

"Or maybe he does. Dragons are very intelligent, according to legends."

I huffed out a sigh. "This is hopeless."

"It's not hopeless, love. He's just a baby. He's curious."

"He's going to destroy our cottage! After everything we went through to fix my shop..." Panic swirled in my chest, choking off my air and halting my words.

"He's not going to destroy anything. The cottage is protected, remember? He's not going to destroy anything." Redd wrapped a reassuring arm around my shoulders, squeezing me into his side. I breathed a little easier.

A tiny voice chimed in from up on the shelf next to the dragon. "It's going to be alright, Fiella!"

I think that sprite was Scarlett. It was actually really nice, having tiny folk around that were always willing to help and reassure at a moment's notice. Kizzi should have been more grateful.

"You think so?" I asked.

"The fates will it, so it will be," she said sagely.

"That sounds very wise," Redd muttered under his breath.

"Just the truth," Scarlett responded.

Redd flinched, clearly not expecting the sprite to be able to hear him from the perch across the room.

We kept forgetting that the sprites were inherently magical, and that none of us really knew what they were capable of.

He cleared his throat. "Right. Well. I guess we should just go about our day as usual?"

"How are we supposed to act normal when we have a fire breathing beast in our cottage?" I wailed.

"We haven't actually seen Ember breathe any fire," Redd said calmly. "He might have to grow into that."

I choked. I hadn't even considered what would happen

when the dragon grew. How big did dragons even get? Would he even fit inside the cottage anymore?

Redd grabbed me by my upper arms, shaking me gently to catch my attention. "Stop spiraling. We can do this. *You* can do this."

"We can't!"

"We can. You wanted this. Just remember how excited you were when Kizzi brought the eggs back. You were meant for this. You know that."

I sniffed. "I was excited," I agreed, my voice unsteady.

"You were *so* excited. Just look at him up there. He's having so much fun."

I did what Redd said, returning my gaze to the dragon perched on my highest shelf. He did look happy. He was watching Hex, where they were curled up on an end table, stiffening into different shapes.

I personally thought the sight of the magical slime was horrifying, but the dragon found it entertaining.

He really was just a baby.

Gathering myself, I straightened, steeling my spine and hardening my nerves. Redd released me but he stayed close, hovering. Prepared to step in at any moment.

I snatched a scrap piece of yarn from one of my knitting projects, tying it to a stick that Sookie had brought inside for some reason.

If cats liked playing with toys, perhaps baby dragons did, too.

Hesitantly, holding my breath, I held the string on a stick out where Ember could see it.

His eyes zeroed in on the string immediately.

"Careful," Redd said to the room in general.

I swallowed. "Here, dragon, dragon, dragon," I called in a high-pitched voice. I waved the stick back and forth, letting the string flutter.

It took a few moments, but it worked.

Ember spread his wings, knocking the bowl and scrolls from the shelf, but he didn't even notice.

He dove.

My scream came out garbled as I slapped my hand over my face, trying to stifle the sound.

I held the stick out as far as my arm would reach, my fingers clamped onto it like iron.

To my surprise, I didn't hear any shattering crash. From the corner of my eye, I watched a group of sprites leap and dip, zipping through the air to catch the falling items, working together to set them back where they belonged.

My relief was short lived, though, because the beast was charging.

Ember, instead of landing on the ground, chose to land directly on my arm.

He damn near plowed me over. I only stayed on my feet because of Redd's sturdy grip on my shoulders.

"Ahh!" I shouted as the dragon latched onto my arm with four clawed feet. Paws? Feet? I wasn't sure.

He wasn't heavy, but he was *strong*. And he was surprisingly agile, nowhere near as wobbly as he had been the night before in Kizzi's shop.

He was growing up so fast.

Strangely, that made me want to cry.

Ember swatted at my hand, which was still clutching the stick. I held fast.

"That's not how you're supposed to play with it!" I called, my voice shaking. "Let me hold it!"

The dragon tilted his head. He swatted at my hand again, harder this time.

"Ouch!" I yelped. "That hurts!"

Redd grumbled behind me, something that sounded like, "Damned beast."

The dragon stilled, turning its head to glance at my face. He snorted.

Then he hopped to the floor, landing with a soft thud.

I exhaled heavily. "There you go," I cooed. "Good dragon. Like *this*."

I wiggled the string again. This time, the dragon tensed and leaped, but he stayed near the floor. He lunged for the string, trying to grasp it in his teeth, but the string slipped away before he could find a solid grip.

I chuckled. It really was like playing with a cat. "Almost! Try again!"

I continued to wiggle the string as the dragon dipped and dodged, swiping over and over again and snapping his teeth with audible clicks.

Redd laughed lowly behind me. I glanced at him. "Want to try?"

"Oh, no, I like watching you do it," he said, but I could see the way his eyebrows quirked with interest.

I shoved the stick into his hand. "Just try it. It's fun."

He looked confused for a moment, but then he hesitantly stuck his arm out, jiggling the string gently.

Ember reacted instantly, this time rolling onto this back and kicking at the string with all four legs.

I laughed louder. "Look at him!" I called. "He's like a bug!"

"Not a bug," Redd said, lifting the stick high above his head. Ember jumped for it. "A beast. A very *smart* beast."

Ember let out a sound somewhere between a purr and a growl. I flinched, but immediately regained my composure.

"The smartest beast in the entire realm," I agreed.

The day flew by as we continued to play with the dragon, finding random items for it to chase around the room.

We also were able to pet the creature as it tired, scratching its smooth belly and its horned head.

Even Sookie and Pumpkin seemed to appreciate the dragon, joining in and wrestling with Ember as they fought for possession of a small wad of paper.

My worries melted away with the hours.

Finally, curled up in bed in Redd's arms with the dragon snuggled up with cats somewhere on the floor, I accepted the fact that we were going to be okay.

"See, I told you we could do this," Redd said against the back of my head, his legs entwined with mine.

I snuggled into his embrace. "Fine, I hate to admit it, but you were right."

And he was right. We could do this.

# CHAPTER 11

# Kizzi

"She's cold!" I shouted, chasing the dragon around the room with a blanket stretched out in front of me. I wanted to wrap her up and snuggle her close.

The second dragon was a lovely sapphire blue color, about the same size as the first dragon, but instead of radiating heat, she seemed to absorb it. Instead of steam wafting from her open mouth, she spat small streams of icy water.

"She's not cold," Tandor said gently. "It's nice and warm in here."

"But she was so cozy in her egg, and now she's out." The dragon jumped out of my reach again, vaulting off of the table and putting a few feet between us. Almost like it was a game. I kept at it.

"She was ready to hatch," he reminded. "She's old enough. And she's inside."

"But, but—" I struggled to find a reason that made sense. "She's not warm like Ember."

Tandor thought about this. "That doesn't mean there's a problem, little witch. She's just different."

I finally stopped chasing the dragon, letting the blanket drop to the floor at my feet. My arms refilled with blood in sweet relief—I'd held them out for way too long. "Wait. She?" I asked.

Tandor shrugged. "You said it first, I just went along with it."

I considered this. I hadn't said it on purpose, it had just come out of my mouth. I intrinsically knew.

My stomach fluttered with glee. It was my turn to be chosen by the fates. They wanted *me* to know.

Tandor smiled, making the same realization. "What's her name, then?" He was perched on a stool, grinding up a few stones with a mortar and pestle to help me restock my supplies. He was much better at it than I was, his muscles making the process much faster.

He was perfectly at ease, for some reason. The panic that followed the hatching of Ember was absent, now that Raine had hatched.

I gasped, slapping a hand over my mouth.

"What is it, little witch? I can tell by your face that it just came to you."

"Raine," I said, awe coloring my voice. "Her name is Raine."

"Raine," Tandor repeated. "A beautiful name for a beautiful dragon. I like it."

"It's perfect," I whispered.

A feeling, deep and overwhelming bloomed in my chest, tightening my veins and warping my thoughts. It was love, I realized. Love—all encompassing, but different from the love I felt for Tandor. Or even Fiella. This was something new entirely.

I knew that I had to keep her. That I had to protect her, no matter what it cost me. That I would do anything for the little blue dragon.

Tandor watched my face, settling the mortar and pestle down and rising to his feet. "We're keeping her, aren't we?"

Silently, I nodded. My eyes pricked, threatening tears. Tandor tugged me into a warm hug, squishing my face into his chest.

I could hear the smile in his voice when he spoke. "I feel it too, Kiz. I feel it too. She's meant to be here with us."

I nodded again, my cheek rubbing against the smooth fabric of his tunic. I allowed him to hold me for long moments, until Raine made a small sound in the corner.

She had hopped into the broken cauldron and was nudging the green egg curiously with her nose. She let out a small whine.

My heart cracked.

"It'll hatch soon, honey," I reassured. "It's okay."

The dragon nudged the egg again, this time scooting it over a few inches.

I drifted to the cauldron, leaning over to stroke my fingers down the dragon's cool, scaled back. "Don't worry, Raine. Just give it some time."

The dragon tensed for a moment, but then she relaxed, leaning into my hand for more pets.

I melted.

"Tandor!" I whispered. "Check this out!"

"I see it," he whispered back. "Look at you go!"

Rain tilted her head, allowing me to scratch her on her hard, scaled chin. "I think she likes me."

"Of course she does. She would be a fool not to."

I flushed, my ears growing warm. "Should I try to pick her up?"

"Go for it. What's the worst that could happen?"

"She could bite my finger off. Or my entire hand, if it would fit in her mouth."

"She's not going to bite your finger off."

"How do you know that?"

"I just know. Now pick her up, or I will."

This steeled my resolve. I knew Raine would favor Tandor, because all critters did. This was my chance to bond with her first. "Okay. If I lose a finger, there's a medical kit in a basket somewhere. Don't let me bleed out."

"I won't let you bleed out, princess." There was a smile in his voice.

Holding my breath, I bent over the lip of the cauldron, scooping the small dragon into my arms.

# CHAPTER 12

# *Fiella*

The days before Merry Day passed in a blur of dragon scales, smoking leaves, and icy puddles.

They were the most exciting and exhausting days of my life. And now, Merry Day was tomorrow, and I was *not* prepared. I had managed to finish my knitted gifts, sure, but I wanted to make them even better. I wanted to make sure they were *perfect*. And I wanted to wrap them up beautifully and intricately. If I found the time, I would.

Ember, surprisingly, had actually been helpful when it came to knitting. When he wasn't too busy chasing Sookie around, he helped me keep strands of yarn from tangling, and if I let him play with the scrap pieces, he even helped me keep my rows and knots straight and even.

I wouldn't have finished the projects without him. I wouldn't admit that, though. It was too embarrassing to say, "The baby dragon is better at knitting than I am," out loud.

The dragons could not be contained indoors. Both my Ember and Kizzi's Raine were relentless in their pursuits for open air, clawing at doors and windows and trying to push through cracks.

After we were pretty sure they weren't actually murderous beasts, we didn't want to contain them. They wanted to explore, and we wanted to make them happy. So, we let them roam.

Mayor Tommins was *not* pleased with that plan.

He had scolded me and Kizzi the first time he saw the two little dragons zipping around Town Square, chasing fluffy squirrels and swatting at crispy, crumpled leaves. He had shouted, and threatened, and even crossed his arms and stared at us disapprovingly (which was the scariest part).

But then, like the rest of us, he fell under their spell. He didn't even yell when Ember caught a pile of leaves on fire dangerously close to his office, or when Raine froze one of the cobblestone paths into a giant icy mess.

He simply laughed, shook his head, and moved along, content to let the dragons play as long as nobody was harmed.

And nobody was harmed, aside from a few slips and singed sleeves. In fact, the entire town was absolutely enthralled.

It was like Kizzi's love potion fiasco all over again, except this time, instead of obsessing over Kizzi, the folk of Moon-vale simply wanted to catch a glimpse of the legendary drag-ons. Or if they were lucky, pet one on their scaly, horned heads.

The third egg—the green one—still hadn't hatched. I wondered what affinity it would have. Would it lean toward flame, like Ember, or would it be drawn to ice, like Raine?

I tried to quell my worry. My stomach churned when I thought about the deal that the witch in Rockward had arranged with Kizzi—if the dragon didn't hatch by Merry Day, we had to return the egg to the mountains.

There was still time. Only a day, but time, nonetheless.

"Hot cocoa?" Redd asked as he dropped onto the bench beside me. I was perched in the park in Town Square, watching Ember and Raine fight over a little stick while a few cats perched on benches nearby, watching the fiasco unfold.

There was no better entertainment.

I grabbed the mug gratefully, relishing the way the heat soaked through my knitted gloves and warmed my stiff fingers. "You're the best. Did you know that?"

He chuckled. "Who's winning?"

I blew on the steaming liquid for a moment before taking a tiny sip. My fangs tapped against the mug. The cocoa was almost hot enough to burn, but not quite—the perfect temperature. It was rich and sweet and smelled almost better than it tasted.

"Raine keeps getting the stick away from Ember, but she's too sweet to run away with it—she just sets it down and lets him take it back. But he always underestimates how sneaky she is, so she is able to snatch it away again."

Redd snorted. "That sounds about right. She's all strategy, he's all strength."

"Mhm. I'm resisting the urge to coach him right now. I don't think he wants my pointers. He wouldn't listen, anyway." Quieter, I said, "I've already tried."

Redd laughed even louder. "I would expect nothing less."

Other folk meandered through the park, staying to watch the dragons for a while before eventually returning to their homes.

Linc, a brown-haired human, stayed the longest, hooting

and hollering and cheering whenever one of the dragons stole the stick again. It was practically a spectator sport.

Velline and Lunette stopped by, too, admiring the dragons and complimenting them on their grace and strength.

Even the coven of witches came by at one point, quietly observing with looks of awe on their faces.

Pride swelled in my chest, almost impossible to contain. I felt I would burst with it.

Redd retreated to finish up his last Merry Day gifts, leaving me bundled up on the bench alone. I pulled my cloak closed even tighter, making sure the hood was snug against my ears. The cold threatened to solidify me.

When the suns eventually slipped below the horizon and the moons took their place, and the air cooled to an almost painful degree, I finally stood from the bench.

My knees were stiff and creaky, protesting the change after sitting for so long. My ass wasn't faring much better.

"Alright, beasts!" I called out. "Bedtime!"

Ember whined, steam whistling out of his nose.

"Don't complain, mister. We can come back tomorrow. I know you're sleepy."

Obediently, Raine flew over to me, landing delicately on top of my head.

I wanted to laugh. Days ago, I would have thought this impossible, sitting in the park with a baby dragon on my head.

But this was life now.

I wandered in the direction of Kizzi's apothecary so I could drop her dragon off first. "Let's go, Em. I've got a bowl of sausage links waiting for you at home."

That got him moving. Ember hurried after us, frantically flapping his wings. "Hungry beast," I muttered under my breath.

Rain stayed on top of my head, content to ride me like a carriage.

When we reached Kizzi's shop, I pulled her door open and nudged the blue dragon inside. She was cold as ice. "Delivery!" I called through the open door. "To the Moons, Kiz!"

Her muffled voice responded, somewhere in the back of the shop. "Thanks, Fi! You're the best. To the suns! See you tomorrow!"

"Can't wait!" I pulled the door shut, a grin plastered onto my face.

Ember took Raine's place on top of my head, his claws gripping the fabric of my hood.

I couldn't help it, my smile grew.

# CHAPTER 13

# Kizzi

Ginger's Pub was cozier than ever.

Needled ever-trees from the mountains were propped in the corners, decorated with trinkets on strings. A fire roared in the hearth, crackling and popping and casting the room in a comfortable, warm glow. Twinkling, enchanted string lights brought a magical glow to the place, warming it even further.

Stacks of presents sat against the far wall, waiting for meals to be finished.

The murmur of voices blended into a soothing symphony, making the place feel lively and joyful.

Merry Day was my favorite day of the entire year.

While many folk chose to celebrate the holiday at home with their loved ones, some of us preferred even more company, so Ginny always welcomed the town into the pub with open arms.

She had prepared a giant vat of stew, chicken and rosemary this time, and the scents of herbs and baked bread mingled happily with the smoke from the fire.

I adjusted my hair, tugging on the bow to make sure it was sitting just right.

We were all wearing our finest outfits. My corset and skirt matched my red shawl perfectly, only accentuated by my red lace-up boots. Fiella's trousers were clean and pressed, and her blue hair was smoothed into a lovely braid that kept the wild strands out of her face. Redd had trimmed his beard down, and his white tunic was bright and wrinkle free. And Tandor looked impossibly handsome in a red sweater that made his green skin look warm and flushed.

We all cleaned up pretty nice, if I could say so myself.

"Another cider for the table?" Tandor asked, standing up and gathering our goblets.

"Yes, please!" I said.

"Thanks!" Fiella responded.

Redd nodded with a smile.

The cranberry cider Tandor had come up with was incredible. It was one of his best yet. Tart, sweet, with just the right amount of cinnamon bite, it was a masterpiece.

It didn't beat the pumpkin, but it was a close second.

"I'll get them!" Ginger called from behind the bar. "Don't worry about it, Tandor!"

Tandor ignored her, bringing the goblets with him. "You've been working all morning, Ginny. Sit. Take a break. I've got this one."

"Oh no, I don't mind," the faun protested, but Tandor would not be deterred. He simply flicked his head in the direction of our table, where an empty chair was waiting for her.

"Sit," he ordered.

This time, she listened. "Fine. But only for a minute." She

scurried over the table, goblet and bowl in hand. She sat down heavily, allowing her weight to drop into the chair without her usual grace.

I leaned over, patting her on the shoulder. "You work too hard."

She smiled around a mouthful of stew. She swallowed, before she said, "Says you."

I sat back in my chair, glancing around the room. We weren't the only patrons in the pub. Velline and Old Man Wilbur were at a table in the corner with a few other folk. A family of shifters occupied another table. Linc sat at the bar with Lunette, who was listening to his animated story with an amused smile on her face. The pub was bustling. "I don't work on holidays," I argued. "I'm too lazy for that."

She grinned, shrugging. "I don't mind. I like taking care of people."

"Fire!" someone shouted from the other side of the room. "It's the dragon!'

My eyes darted in that direction, but a tiny voice near my ear said, "I'm on it, Godsblood."

It was Dropp, the water sprite. The sprites had taken to following me around town, becoming more familiar with Moonvale. It seemed that they were no longer confined to my shop, if they ever were in the first place. They spent most of their time in my apothecary, but they were beginning to wander.

I was so proud of them. My little menaces.

"Thanks, you're the best!" I called out.

Ember had caught a napkin on fire, and Dropp easily extinguished the flame with a small stream of water.

If only Raine would do that. The two dragons could keep

each other in check if they chose to, but instead, they seemed to compound on each other's shenanigans.

"That is so convenient," Fiella muttered.

"Sure is," Tandor agreed as he returned to the table, goblets in hand. He passed the drinks around the table before returning to his seat between me and Ginger. The chair groaned when his weight settled onto it.

"Godsblood? Why did she call you that?" Ginger asked, confused.

I flapped my hand dismissively. "I'm not sure, but they won't stop."

"It's because she's the Godsblood, of course," another sprite chimed in. Scarlett. She was sitting on the table, staring longingly at the rest of the stew in my bowl. I nudged it toward her.

I shrugged. "Whatever that means."

Ginger stared at me for a moment before she simply nodded, returning her attention to her own bowl of stew. "It's a cool name."

"It's a ridiculous name," I argued.

"I think it's kind of funny," Fiella chimed in from across the table.

"Nobody asked you," I grumbled, but it had no bite to it.

She snorted a laugh in response. "Grumpy. Will some gifts break you out of your bad attitude?"

I straightened. "Maybe."

Anticipation fluttered in my chest. I was nervous to give my gifts to the others. I had spent a lot of time on them, and I was pretty sure they would be appreciated, but I was feeling wobbly, nonetheless.

Ginger scarfed down the rest of her stew before rising, her

hoofed feet clacking against the stone floor. "Let me clear these bowls away first."

Tandor beat her to it, snatching the bowls with impressive speed. "Sit, boss."

With a roll of her eyes, she sat. she leaned back and crossed her ankles, her cheek twitching but not quite forming a smile.

As Tandor cleared the dishes away from the table, leaving us with just our goblets, Redd brought the gift boxes to us.

Mayor Tommins stood to leave from where he sat in the back of the room, brushing his hands off on his trousers and drifting toward the door.

"Going somewhere?" Fiella asked.

"I think I'll head to bed," he said, voice tight. "I'm tired."

I shook my head. "Stay, Tommins. It's Merry Day." I kicked at the chair to my right that was unoccupied. "At least have a cider. This cranberry flavor is incredible."

He hesitated, his jaw working. He seemed conflicted.

"Stay," Redd urged. "Just for a bit. It's too early to go to sleep, even for you."

Slowly, the gryphon nodded. "I suppose one drink wouldn't kill me."

He settled into the chair next to me, his back ramrod straight and his hands folded on the table in front of him. Tandor set a goblet down, and he grasped it quickly, seemingly grateful to have something to hold onto.

I smiled. He was nervous. It was kind of sweet.

"So, Tommins. Any big plans for Moonvale in the coming months?" I asked to try to ease his tension.

It worked. He relaxed slightly as he took a sip of cider. "If those monsters don't destroy it first, you mean?" he asked, gesturing to the dragons who were now curled up in front of the fireplace.

"Precisely," I said sarcastically.

He considered this. "With magic returning, I don't know what to expect. I'm hoping the next few months are completely uneventful, if I'm being honest."

"Uneventful is boring!" Fiella griped.

"Boring is safe," Tommins insisted. "Boring is good."

Redd tilted his head as he settled back into his chair. "I can't disagree with you there."

The table was now full of boxes and bags of varying sizes. Gifts both big and small cluttered the space. I could hardly see Fiella across the table.

Tommins looked for a moment like he would flee, but I patted him on the shoulder, sending a small zap of magic into him. He flinched, and then glared at me.

"You don't have to leave," I insisted.

"I don't want to intrude—"

I shook my head. "Nobody thinks you're intruding."

"But you're all friends, and I'm..." He trailed off, unsure.

"You're our friend, too," Fiella said warmly. "Even if you do threaten to send us to the dungeon a little too often."

Mayor Tommins' face flushed, dark and warm. He cleared his throat twice before he spoke again. "Well, someone has to keep you crazy folk in check."

Fiella raised her goblet, a broad grin baring her fangs. "I'll cheers to that."

We all lifted our glasses. Tommins looked bashful, but he raised his glass, too.

"And cheers to Merry Day!" Ginger added before she took a long swallow from her glass. She set it down with a thunk and then leaned back, kicking her hooves up and resting them on the edge of the table. If it were anyone else, we would've gotten a thump on the back of the head, but being the pub owner had its perks. "Now, who's first! Redd!"

Redd startled. "Me? Oh, no. Someone else."

"Redd! Redd!" Fiella chanted.

The rest of us joined in. "Redd! Redd!"

His cheeks darkened. "Oh fine, fine." Under his breath, he grumbled, "I'll get it over with."

I glanced at Fiella from the corner of my eye to find her absolutely beaming. Lovesick fool. I suppressed my own grin.

Redd had three packages in front of him. He opened them with a brisk efficiency.

The first package, from Fiella, contained two items. The first was a knitted hat, striped with varying lines of brown and green. It was actually pretty nice. The second item was harder to work out.

He held the bundle up questioningly. "I love it," he said warmly. Then he cleared his throat. "But... what is it?"

Fiella snorted. "It's a strap for your tools! You can wrap it around your waist, and it'll carry your hammers and mallets, so you don't have to bend all the way to the ground to retrieve them from your toolbox."

Redd stared at her with soft eyes, his jaw working. "It's perfect," he said. His voice was husky.

Fiella was absolutely radiant. "You like it?"

"I love it."

"Save the lovey dovey stuff for your cottage!" I complained. "Open mine next!"

Redd cleared his throat, glancing around the room as though remembering he had an audience. "Right. Of course."

He pulled the top off of the box, and then smiled. "Is this what I think it is?"

"If you think it's enchanted sandpaper that can smooth even the toughest of wood in mere seconds, then you'd be correct!" I declared.

He nodded in my direction. "This is amazing. I didn't even know enchantments like that were possible. Thank you."

I brushed it off. "It's easy, now that the magic is back, and all that. No big deal." But secretly, I was pleased.

His next gift was a collection of tiny knives from Tandor that would be perfect for carving critters out of wood, just like his Pa. Redd had actually been speechless at that gift. Tandor had thumped him on the back, insisting that Redd had to make him a dragon sculpture first.

And then it was my turn to open gifts.

Fiella had knitted me a giant blanket that was unbelievably plush, and by far the softest thing I had ever touched. My awe was impossible to contain. "You made this?" I gasped, stroking my fingers over the even loops and swirls.

She nodded smugly. "I sure did. It'll keep you warm while you're reading those raunchy—"

I interrupted her before she could embarrass me in front of Mayor Tommins. "I love it! I didn't realize you were a knitting expert."

She laughed it off, but I could tell she was happy about the praise. Fiella loved a compliment more than anyone.

Tandor's gift wasn't something he could hand over, but it was something even better.

He had worked with the witches and the farmers and figured out how to grow pumpkins in Moonvale, right on the edge where the Barren Lands met the Greenwood Forest. He promised to make me pumpkin ciders year-round.

I had actually teared up at that one. I threw myself at him, wrapping him in the biggest hug I could muster.

And Redd and Ginger had worked together to make me a plant stand that would elevate the pots, allowing me to cram even more of them in front of my shop windows. It was perfect.

And then it was Tandor's turn.

He received a sweater that had "I love critters!" stitched onto the front, along with a giant barrel, larger than any of the others in the pub, for brewing his ciders. Ginger had to teach us how to make the barrel acceptable for brewing, fixing it up and adding the necessary attachments. He was ecstatic. The orc had gone around the room, pulling everyone into a bear hug. Even Mayor Tommins, who accepted the hug with a bewildered look on his face.

And then it was time for Fiella to open her gifts. The boxes on the table began to dwindle.

The first was from me. She opened it, and then smiled. "A goblet! Wow, it's gorgeous. Is that my name engraved on the front?"

"It's enchanted. So your drinks will never get cold."

Her jaw dropped. "No fucking way."

"Yes fucking way!"

She had squealed with excitement, immediately transferring the remnants of her cider into the new goblet to test it out.

Tandor and Redd rose, slipping to the back room. They returned, each lugging a huge gift in front of them.

Fiella cried out, slapping her hands over her mouth. "Is that what I think it is?"

Redd smiled, glancing at Tandor, who was also grinning. "Your own barrel of lavender blueberry cider. It'll stay here, of course, but it'll always be filled," Tandor said.

Redd tore the paper from his own gift. Gasps echoed around the room. It was a mailbox, similar to the ones in town, but made of wood instead of stone. On the front was her shop name, Fiella's Finds. He had made Fiella her own mailbox.

We were all familiar with how they liked to correspond by letter, even now.

It was way better than my gift, damn it. I could admit when I had been defeated.

Fiella had promptly burst into tears, of course. She sobbed, blubbering out unintelligible thanks to the men.

As the chattering died down, Mayor Tommins cleared his throat. "I have a gift for you folk," he said quietly, reaching into his pocket. He pulled out three bells. One red, one blue, one green. He set them on the table in front of him. "They are dragon bells. Kizziah, you might have to lay an enchantment over them, but they should be able to summon your dragon, no matter how far they wander."

Again, I was fighting tears. Tommins, who was so resistant to the dragons at first, had now found a way to ensure that we would never lose the dragons again.

I couldn't wait until Tommins could see his own gift, which was a massive wooden sign that read, "Welcome to Moonvale, The Heart of Magic." Redd had already told him that he would have to wait until morning to see it, under the light of the two suns.

I caught Fiella's eye and nodded, signaling that it was time.

Time for the final gift.

I bent, retrieving the last box from beneath the table. I set it down carefully, sliding it to Ginger. She sat up straight, looking flustered. "Oh, you didn't have to—"

"Just open it, Ginny," Fiella interrupted. She was actually vibrating with excitement, bouncing on the balls of her feet. A glance around the room told me that Redd and Tandor were just as excited.

She looked at us suspiciously. "What is it?"

"Open it!" I ordered.

With a heavy sigh, she pulled the lid off the box.

And then she promptly shut it again, shoving it in my direction. "No."

"Yes!" I insisted.

"No way. I'm not worthy."

"Yes, you are, Ginny," Fiella said. "You deserve it more than any of us."

I lifted the lid to peer inside, and nearly jumped out of my skin.

In the box, nestled into a small blanket and sleeping peacefully, was a tiny green dragon, surrounded by the fragments of his broken shell. He had hatched sometime during the festivities and was apparently content to nap until he was disturbed. He peeked an eye open, glanced around, and then shut it again before resuming a sleepy breathing rhythm.

Tears ran down Ginger's freckled cheeks. "Are you sure?"

"What's his name, Ginny?" I asked to prove a point.

She sniffled. "Brambleby. His name is Brambleby, or

Bramble, for short. He doesn't mind Bram, either. Why do I know that?"

"Because he's yours, girl!" I shouted. "I told you!"

She stood, gathering me into a tight hug that squeezed the air of my chest. "Thank you," she whispered into my ear. "You have no idea how much this means to me."

I patted her back. "I might have some idea." I pulled back and wiped the tear tracks from her face. "Now, let that baby sleep, because he'll be a handful when he wakes up!"

After many tearful hugs and heartfelt thanks around the room, my heart was fuller than ever before. It felt near to bursting.

Even Hex and the cats had snuck in while we were exchanging gifts, curling up in front of the fireplace with the sprites and the dragons.

My makeshift zoo, growing day by day.

As the day transformed into dusk, and then to night, folk trickled out, donning their cloaks and saying their joyful farewells as they went.

But our group remained, drinking and laughing and simply enjoying the company.

It was the perfect evening.

Until a knock sounded at the door. Which was weird, considering it wasn't locked.

"Come in!" Tandor called, his deep voice booming in the large room.

Nothing happened.

"It's open!" he yelled again, louder this time.

Still, nobody entered.

With a groan, Ginger rose. She clomped to the door with exaggerated slowness.

Ginger pulled the door open, planting her hands on her hips. Cold air rushed in around her, but her body blocked the guest from view. "Can I help you?" she asked.

For a while, there was no response. Ginger tapped her hoof against the floor impatiently. "Well?" she asked.

A voice, strong and deep, slipped around Ginger and filled the room. The sound was an echo that rattled the walls and made the hairs on my arms stand on end. The words the stranger spoke made no sense.

Ginger gasped in outrage, stepping back and stammering, "Excuse me? No, you're thinking of someone else. Sorry."

She tried to slam the door shut, but the stranger stuck a hand out, blocking it.

What did he say? His words had been wondrous, spoken with awe and delivered with a power that was undeniable. I slapped my hand over my mouth to stifle the gasp that tried to rip free.

The words had been an enigma.

"*My mate.*"

Ginger sure was having an eventful day.

# Also by Hailey Blackwood

The Moonvale Matches Series

#1: Love Letters and Thirst Tonics

#2: Cauldrons and Cat Tails

#2.5: Merry in Moonvale

#3: Shadows and Ciders

Moonvale Matches #4 Coming Late 2025

# About the Author

Hailey Blackwood is a lover of all things fantasy—from cozy to dark and everywhere in between. She has always been an avid reader, but she has stepped into the author world with her debut novel, Love Letters and Thirst Tonics, the sequel, Cauldrons and Cat Tails, and the holiday novella, Merry in Moonvale. When Hailey is not reading or writing, you will probably find her drinking tea (or wine) at home surrounded by her four cats and multitude of houseplants. She loves magical creatures, wholesome MMCs, and cozy fantasy worlds that you feel like you can step right into.

www.authorhaileyblackwood.com

instagram.com/authorhaileyblackwood
tiktok.com/@authorhaileyblackwood
amazon.com/author/haileyblackwood

www.ingramcontent.com/pod-product-compliance
Lightning Source LLC
Chambersburg PA
CBHW030008010826
48973CB00009B/2717